Praise for *The Vanishing Season*

"Anderson once again works her magic to conjure evocative settings and soulful protagonists in this modern gothic romance. This tantalizing novel offers a singular perspective on a complicated love triangle and a tragedy."

—*Publishers Weekly* (starred review)

"This is a book to be read twice through, once for the sweetly tragic love story and mystery, and a second time for the subtle imagery and metaphorical connections. The three protagonists are all achingly lovable as they seek to act nobly and preserve kindness in an impossible situation."

—*BCCB* (starred review)

"A heartbreaking story full of mystery, love, redemption, and betrayal." —*SLJ* (starred review)

"For readers who savor the ambiguities of unrequited love and the grays of the here and hereafter." — *VOYA*

"An intensely gripping tale with a surprise ending that's fully earned." —*Kirkus Reviews*

"Readers who like their romances tragic and dreamy should dive in." —ALA *Booklist*

Also by Jodi Lynn Anderson

Peaches
The Secrets of Peaches
Love and Peaches

Tiger Lily

THE VANISHING SEASON

JODI LYNN ANDERSON

An Imprint of HarperCollinsPublishers

Library of Congress Control Number: 2014934799
ISBN 978-0-06-200328-7

Typography by Torborg Davern
15 16 17 18 19 CG/RRDH   10 9 8 7 6 5 4 3 2 1

First paperback edition, 2015

Even the open, transparent lake has
its unknown depths, which no divers know.

—HANS CHRISTIAN ANDERSEN

THE
VANISHING
SEASON

A key is buried under the front stairs of 208 Water Street. Scorched on one side—was it in a fire? Who lost it and when?

For me it's a clue, a piece of the past. Because the yard of this house is a graveyard of moments, and everything left behind is a reminder: sandpaper, a bracelet, a love note, some letters, a match, a movie ticket stub, a postcard. All of Door County is a burial ground. All of the world. And I am here to dig.

It seems that this town has an appetite for the young; it swallows them whole, right into its very dirt.

A key is buried under the front stairs on Water Street.

This is my work. This is the one thing I have to do.

I am looking for the things that are buried.

1

THE LARSENS FIRST READ ABOUT THE MURDERS ON A MID-SEPTEMBER EVENING in Maggie's senior year of high school, the day they moved to Gill Creek. This was the first time it began to feel like something was looming near them, a little bit off on the horizon. It was also the first day Maggie saw Pauline Boden. She was standing at the lake's edge and leaning against a boulder, as skinny as a stork, staring out at the water.

"Someone your age," Maggie's mom crooned, pointing across the vast, overgrown field that separated their house from the lake to the thin, white figure on the bank. Maggie looked to her mom in exasperation—they were both out of breath and lugging their suitcases across the yard, but even so, her mom hadn't given up her relentless mission to point out the positives.

Maggie dropped her box of linens in front of the porch stairs and surveyed their new house, thinking her mother had her mission cut out for her.

Her uncle had described the property, which they'd inherited years ago, as "rustic." In pictures it had looked run-down. In person it was closer to "ramshackle" or "derelict." They'd never even bothered to come look at it, always planning to sell it when they got around to it—but things had been different then.

Maggie stood with her hands on her hips and tried to catch her breath, sweat dripping down her temples. They'd already lugged a bunch of boxes onto the front porch, but they hadn't even started on the furniture in the U-Haul yet. They couldn't afford movers, so she tried to look like she didn't mind the work. Now she pulled out her cell phone to see if she had any texts, but there was no signal. She looked around for some kind of hill where she might get better reception, but the land was flat and low to the water. She felt a pang for her friends back home.

Mrs. Larsen rested her hands on her hips too and stared around at the yard. "It'll take some work, but it really is beautiful. Don't you think, Maggles?"

Truthfully the property *was* beautiful, in a shabby, romantic, old-fashioned way. The house, a yellowing, formerly white Victorian, looked ancient and barely livable. "Built in 1886," her dad had said. It slumped on a wide expanse of tall, browning, late-summer grass that stretched to the shore of

Lake Michigan under an expanse of endless blue sky. The grass was alive with grasshoppers twirling from one landing spot to the next, and already Maggie could hear the crickets coming awake. Crickets were a novelty. She'd only ever lived in Chicago, falling asleep to city sounds almost every night for as long as she could remember.

Making the spot even more serene was the fact that the adjoining property—the one that must belong to the girl on the beach—was spectacular. You could tell where one lot ended and the other began by the deeply green, manicured lawn that started at the property line. A majestic, gleaming white house stood just at the lake's edge, about a hundred yards from the Larsens' new front door and partially obscured by a thin forest of pine trees.

"It's great," Maggie said, giving her mom her best "can-do" smile. This was her permanent facial expression these days, whenever she looked at her parents. She wanted them to know that, whatever problems they were dealing with right now, *she* wasn't going to be one of them.

"Have you seen your room?" her dad asked, heaving his way up the stairs with a box of books in his arms, his balding head glistening in the sun.

Maggie shook her head. She hadn't even gone inside yet, dropping boxes on the porch, though her parents had gone in several times already. It was her way of putting off the inevitable reality of a new home and a new life she didn't want. But now she faked excitement and followed him inside.

The interior was covered with a thin layer of dust, and the floors were slightly bowed in the middle, everything wooden and antique and distressed-looking. The kitchen appliances were mustard yellow but the walls were a faded pastel, as if the seventies had vomited all over the fifties. Little artifacts from previous residents lay scattered here and there: a domino on the kitchen floor, a coupon stuck to the refrigerator by a Mickey Mouse magnet. Maggie continued through the kitchen into the living room, which looked out across a crumbling deck toward the blue shimmer of the lake. Turning left toward another open archway, she walked through a web that she had to pick out of her mouth, then moved on down the hall to the stairs.

She laid her hand on the wobbly banister and creaked her way up to the second floor. To her left she found what she instantly knew would be her room: a nook with a slanted ceiling and a large window that looked out on the grass and across it toward the white house, with a small, yellowing radiator against one wall. The cozy space felt like a hideaway from the world and smelled like trapped summer air, flowery and dusty.

It made her think of the Dashwoods in *Sense and Sensibility*, downgrading to a cottage by the sea. She could make the best of it, like they had. And if life ended up being as underwhelming here as she expected . . . well, it was only a year anyway—then graduation, then *real* life.

She walked back downstairs and onto the back deck,

where her parents were taking a breather on an ancient porch swing that looked like it would collapse at any moment. Her dad had bought a local paper on their way through town, and he handed her the piece he was done with already. "We're taking a ten-minute break," he said. "Absorb some local flavor." He smiled at her—his apologetic "I'm sorry we're putting you through this" smile. Maggie took the paper—not because she wanted to read it but because she wanted to be obliging.

She sat on the top step of the porch and flipped through the back pages of the section first (a habit), reading about a fishing captain who restored old ships and the latest public appearances of the Princess of the Cherry Festival and a fender bender in Sturgeon Bay. She and her dad exchanged an amused glance; the paper was almost painfully quaint.

But on the front page was a story about a teenager who'd died in Whitefish Harbor, four towns over. (Maggie remembered driving past it once they'd arrived on the peninsula.) The girl had been found drowned in the lake, floating facedown with no signs of a struggle, and the police were trying to figure out whether it was a suicide, an accident, or something more sinister.

"Anything interesting, you two?" her mom asked.

"A girl died," Maggie said to her mom. "They think she may have killed herself."

Mrs. Larsen put her hand to her throat, looking slightly sickened. "Oh, how awful. Her poor parents."

Maggie looked up from her paper and saw the skinny

girl along the shore finally turning and walking toward her house.

"Probably pretty unheard of in a small town like that," her dad said. "What a shock."

"Well," her mom said, after letting out a long sigh, "the sun'll be down in about an hour. No rest for the wicked. Let's get the rest of this stuff inside."

Maggie stood without a complaint. Her mom always said she was the world's only teenager who never complained about anything.

2

MAGGIE AWOKE THE NEXT MORNING TO THE DISTANT SOUND OF HAMMERING IN the woods. She sat up, stretched, pressed her face against the window, and looked down across the field toward the trees with the sun warming her face. She got out of bed.

Her dad was on the back porch, his hands on his hips, looking around in confusion. It only took a moment to see why. The railings of their crumbling porch were covered in vases of wildflowers and boxes of . . . Maggie stepped closer to examine one . . . Earl Grey tea. There had to be at least twenty boxes of tea, covering every available surface of the railing. Running her hands along some of the flowers, she finally came to a white envelope taped to one of the vases. Inside was a blank white card with one line scrawled in wild, messy cursive at the center: *Welcome to Water Street.*

She and her dad exchanged an amused, bewildered smile.

"Friendly," her dad said.

"And weird," Maggie added.

There was no signature.

"Well, hopefully they'll come by again," her dad said, then yawned. "What a place," he said. "Porte des Morts. At least we made it through our first night." He widened his eyes in mock relief.

An hour south of here—Maggie knew from studying the map they had in the car—the peninsula of Door County forked off from Wisconsin like a hitchhiker's thumb into the lake, isolating itself. The whole county—according to the guidebooks her dad had piled onto her lap in the car— was full of unspoiled marshes and pebbly beaches; low, gray rock cliffs along the slate-blue waterline; piney forests; old lighthouses; ancient drive-ins; and old-fashioned motels. Below the county line, the cities left the peninsula alone (outside of the summer months at least, when tourists poured in to rent summer cottages and eat their body weight in fudge and cheese curds). But the most interesting thing she'd read was the reason for the county's name. The French had christened it Porte des Morts, or Death's Door, because the strait between Door County and the mainland was littered with shipwrecks—supposedly more than in any other section of freshwater in the world. Several things made the straits dangerous, apparently: hidden underwater shoals, unpredictable winds, and storms.

"I like Earl Grey," her dad said, and started gathering up the tea. "It makes me feel British."

That week, when they weren't doing her homeschool lessons, Maggie and her dad tried to get the house into livable order while her mom started her new job at the Gill Creek Community Bank. It was a huge step down from her executive job at the bank in Chicago, but it had been the best she could find. Maggie would have to find a job too. She'd been painstakingly saving for college since the day her mom had been laid off the first time, three years ago.

Each morning Maggie put on an old pair of overalls she'd found at Goodwill and scrubbed one room from top to bottom—spreading suds all over the wooden floors of the kitchen, living room, parlor, and hallway, while her dad tinkered at this and that counter or banister or door that needed fixing, learning to be a handyman as he went, with a big book he'd bought at Lowe's by his side. The house began to reveal itself under its layers of dirt: delicately flowered linoleum from the forties or fifties, pale pastel walls, ancient scratches in the floor. Maggie even found the name *Kitty* carved messily into the back of the medicine cabinet and dated 1890, as if some little girl had been determined to leave her mark on the place.

The weather was warm, but the heat of summer was gone, so they left all the doors open, ignoring the few bugs that flew in through the holes in the screens. As Maggie worked she could hear the distant lapping of the water on the lakeshore and, sometimes, the distant hammering in the woods. She still hadn't taken the time to walk over to the lake and dip a toe in.

She scrubbed, dusted, and arranged her room bit by bit. The walls were a flaking sprawl of pink flowers, which she peeled using a scraper and hot water mixed with fabric softener. Once that was done, she painted the walls a pale blue that her dad picked up on sale at Lowe's, which looked much better but also too plain. She dug out her pencils and a piece of loose-leaf and sat down to sketch a mural to do on one wall. But after sitting for a while, tapping her pencil against her teeth, she couldn't think of anything that she was really excited about. She decided to wait for inspiration to strike, if ever. Maggie had used to paint and draw all the time as a kid. She'd been good at it, but over the past few years her enthusiasm for it had slipped away.

Once the plain white shelves were immaculately clean, she filled them with photos of her and Jacie, her and her parents, her favorite books (*Jane Eyre, One Flew Over the Cuckoo's Nest, Beloved*), her dusty sketchbook that she hadn't opened in years, and a figurine of a spider on a web that reminded her of *Charlotte's Web* (which had been her favorite when she was a kid). She put a standing lamp in the corner so that it dimly illuminated her bed for reading, and tucked her white coverlet tight around the edges of her mattress the way she liked it. She put her collection of paints and canvases in a low cabinet, at the back, where they were unlikely to see the light of day again.

That evening she finally got to put on her running shoes, pull her long hair into a ponytail, and jog down Water Street—which was the one way in and out and stretched across two miles of mostly empty fields and woods before it hit a main road. It all looked different running than from the car: the dipping valley; the pastures; the shimmer of the line of Lake Michigan to her left; the stand of thick, shady pine trees across the fields. From some slight rises along the road she could see the shining tin tops of distantly neighboring farmhouses, but when she pulled out her cell phone there was still no signal. Besides the house next door, there was only one more property, obscured within the woods and marked by a rusted, crooked mailbox with a No Trespassing sticker stuck to one side, a Beware of Dog sign planted beside it, and a long, winding driveway that disappeared into the trees. It had to be the property where the hammering had been coming from, but she didn't slow down to get a closer look.

Her blood was pumping hard now. Every time she got a glimpse of the sky, it seemed to be doing something different: filling up with white, puffy clouds; getting crisscrossed and scarred by the trails of airplanes; graying and seemingly getting lower to the ground. Running, Maggie liked to imagine she was a buck, strong and fast. It always made her feel less restless, a little less stuck in her own skin. She pushed herself, going harder than usual. At the end of her route, panting and holding her knees, she paused to look at a tall, gray silo in a field of high grass, and the sky lit up for a split second. A late-summer storm was coming in, and the silo stood out stark white against the gray night. Maggie turned back. She knew, from the ride in (she hadn't been away from Water Street since), that there was nothing for another mile but wilderness.

Back home her dad had disappeared into what he had deemed the study, no doubt arranging his over-the-top collection of books (he had over a thousand of them and hadn't been willing to toss even one, much to her mom's despair) in alphabetical order on the sagging, built-in shelves. An obsession with their books was one of the things Maggie and her dad had in common. Also they looked alike—symmetrical, dark-haired, with faint freckles over their noses—though Maggie, he liked to say, was prettier and not as bald. He hadn't had a full-time job in two years, ever since they'd decided to homeschool her. According to him her classes hadn't been keeping up with her brain, even after she'd skipped a grade.

The house was silent and dim from the coming storm. Maggie showered, changed, then grabbed a book at random from a pile by the study door and took it out onto the back porch to watch the dark clouds blowing in. She'd tried to avoid these moments of sitting still all week; these were the times she found herself getting overwhelmed by homesickness. Now she was thinking that she'd never sleep in her apartment again, never spend Saturday mornings in cafés with her best friend, Jacie, talking over lattes. It was an unsettling, weightless feeling, at sixteen, to have everything she'd known her whole life end so abruptly.

The book she'd picked—she saw, glancing at the cover—was nonfiction; it was about butterflies and moths. She flipped through the pages, reading snippets and only half paying attention.

Suddenly a voice to her right startled her. Maggie jerked and turned.

"Sorry, I scared you?"

The girl stood with one foot uncertainly on the bottom stair of the porch; she was wiry, all gazelle-like limbs and long, unkempt, deep-brown hair. She had something—some kind of moving, squirming thing—in her hands. A big, rangy, slobbery hound dog was trailing along behind her. It was the girl Maggie had seen from far away that first day, on the beach.

"Pauline," she said, stretching out her fisted hands as if to shake Maggie's. Maggie leaned forward in her chair. Pauline turned to her dog. "This is Abe, my soul twin." She freed one hand again and patted Abe's snout.

Pauline climbed up the stairs now more confidently and peered into the house curiously. "You know, I always think of this as the haunted house. I'm glad you're here; you'll chase out the ghosts," she said, turning back and coming to sit beside Maggie, without waiting for an invitation.

"I mean, it's not like I really think there are ghosts. I'm not stupid. But it's hard not to wonder. I've seen lights on over here sometimes."

Maggie didn't believe in ghosts. She'd read somewhere that sightings of ghosts were the result of magnetic fields. Or carbon monoxide poisoning in old houses. Pauline jerked open her hands to reveal a duckling.

"I'm taking it to the shelter, but I thought you might like to see it. Crazy, a duckling born this time of year. Maybe its mother left it behind." Pauline stroked the duckling's head gently, a little longingly, with her skinny thumbs. "Ducklings are so cute, they make my eyes water. Do you ever have that happen?" Maggie shook her head. "Where'd you move from?"

"Chicago," Maggie said, unsure of what to make of her new, duckling-loving neighbor.

"Moving must suck."

Maggie wasn't really willing to say whether it sucked or not to someone she didn't know, but Pauline didn't wait for an answer anyway.

"It's a small town, but it's okay. It's boring, but . . ." Pauline stared around, gesturing to the lake. "There's stuff to do on the water. Summer's great except for all the tourists. Winter feels like it will never end. But besides that . . ."

Pauline turned in her seat toward Maggie and pulled up her knees. She shifted the duckling to one hand and held out a long thread of her hair against Maggie's with the other. "Almost the same color," she said. Pauline's was longer and messier, while Maggie's was neatly combed. "Sorry, I don't mean to be overly enthusiastic. I'm just glad you're here. We've never had a neighbor on this side."

Maggie was used to girls like Pauline—strikingly beautiful girls—being a little aloof. Pauline was the opposite; she came across as sweet, eager, and a little lonely. She gazed around at the crumbling deck, then smiled brightly at Maggie.

"Did you get the tea?"

"Yeah, thanks . . . I've never gotten . . . tea as a present before."

"My mom's family has a tea company, Tidings Tea. So we get a ton for free." Maggie had seen the brand in grocery stores; she'd seen ads for it on TV. Tidings Tea was a big deal.

"Wow."

Pauline seemed to sense she was overwhelming Maggie, and she sank back, stretched like a cat, and lapsed into silence for a few moments, studying the yard and the lake and then the house.

Maggie tried to think of something to ask her. Finally she said the first thing that came to her. "What's all the hammering in the woods?" she asked. "Beyond your house?"

Pauline seemed to puzzle over this for a second, and then her eyes lit up with recognition. "Oh, that's my Liam, Liam Witte, our neighbor on the other side, but much farther down

Water Street. He's our age. He's building something between our houses, so we can meet there in the winter." She wrapped her arms around her knees. "He knows I hate the winter, and he says it's a surprise and I'm not allowed to go back there. You should definitely go and say hi."

"That's really sweet." Maggie knew guys were always quick to do favors for beautiful girls. Not that she didn't benefit from the rule now and then, but she wasn't nearly Pauline-beautiful. Girls who were Pauline-beautiful, Maggie knew, had the world open up its gates for them wherever they went. Girls like Maggie were noticed once people looked closely, but most people didn't look that close.

"It's just me and Liam. And the adults. You should come canoeing with us this Sunday afternoon, before the weather turns cold. It'll happen faster than you think."

"I can't swim," Maggie said. She didn't add that she hated water in general. She'd always had a fear of drowning.

"We won't swim," Pauline reassured her, as if the trip were already decided. She asked if Maggie had read about the girl they'd found in the lake.

"Yeah," Maggie said. "Sad."

"Scary," Pauline said, low. She pushed her wild hair back over her shoulders from where it had crept against the sides of her face. "They haven't found who did it."

"I thought it was an accident or suicide or something."

Pauline shook her head. "They said that at first. But no.

My cousin in Sturgeon Bay knows a cop. They just haven't released it in the papers yet."

Maggie felt a chill run down through her feet. "That's horrible."

Suddenly Abe planted his paws on the swing and licked the duckling.

Pauline let out a laugh—so screechy it could scrape paint off a car. That was the first moment Maggie started to like Pauline—the moment she heard her rough, husky laughter that wasn't beautiful at all.

"Well," Pauline said, standing, peering up at the sky as the first drops fell, "I'm gonna take this little guy to the shelter before it pours. Come over anytime. And welcome to the neighborhood, blah-blah-blah."

"Okay, thanks," Maggie said, standing.

Pauline waved over her shoulder as she walked down the stairs. Rather than taking the driveway to the road, she waded straight toward her house through the tall grass, parting it as she went and leaving a river of flinging grasshoppers and Abe bounding behind her.

That night, as heavy rain streaked the windows and thunderclouds settled over the house, Maggie was exploring the small, empty back parlor for remnants of past residents (all she found was a matchbox) when she stepped on a rotten plank and broke through a hole in the floor. For a terrifying moment, one leg dangled into the emptiness of the cellar below the house, the cool, stale air running up her leg. Catching her breath, she yanked her leg out and found her dad in his study, sitting cross-legged on the floor arranging his shelves.

"My foot broke through the floor. I almost died," she teased. But she was shaken.

"So you're saying you want to be able to walk around your own house without feeling that your life's endangered." He nodded, his glasses glinting in the lamplight. "Okay, I can do that, but it seems a little demanding." Maggie smirked at him.

He promised to go into town and buy some supplies the next morning to fix the floor. Then he stood, put his hands on her cheeks, and rubbed them hard, something he'd done ever since she was little. It was his weird dad way of showing affection.

Maggie crawled into bed that night feeling more at home than she had the night before. Knowing one person made more of a difference than she would have guessed. She liked Pauline already. It usually took her longer to form an opinion of people.

Unable to sleep, she peered out into the dark yard. Across the field yellow light from the white house's windows shone through the rain, giving off a comforting sense of safety and the feeling that someone else was out there in the world besides just her and her parents.

Maggie dreamed that night about the lake, black and shining in the dark, with angels spreading their wings on its surface. Open and closed, open and closed, like the wings of moths.

I'm part of this house, and the residents can hear me in their sleep. I rattle the dishes and creak along the floors in the dark. I turn on the lights downstairs, though they're sure they turned them off when they went to bed. I watch a leg crash through the ceiling into the darkness and I reach out to touch it. But I have no hands, no arms, nothing I can see. I wonder if I ever did.

All I know for sure is that I'm timeless: I drift in and out of the past as easily as if I were walking from one room to another. Moments reach out and pull me in. Without meaning to, I've visited centuries in this very same spot. I've watched the building of ships in the harbor. I see things in colors that couldn't possibly be. (The past has a shimmer. Different moments and feelings are colored differently.) I can hear the motion of stars above the house. This is what a haunting is like for the one who haunts—it's like being everywhere and nowhere at once. Time layers on itself, present and past. But this is what time keeps bringing me back to: this house, this peninsula, these people, this girl. It seems I'm stuck to Door County and pinned to Water Street. I can move over other towns, but I end up back here—as if a magnet's pulled me home. And I don't know why.

I search my soul for what I know about ghosts, though I can't remember where I learned it or who I was when I did. Ghosts come back for revenge, or they linger to protect someone, or they stay because of some unfinished business. And I wonder, if I'm a ghost, which kind of ghost am I?

Every day I wait for heaven to open its pearly gates or for a great white light to swallow me. But nothing yet. It makes me think—or maybe only hope—that there's something I am here to do.

I've been noticing moths lately. They seem to congregate wherever I am, alighting on my invisible frame. Outside the cellar window, I watch the souls of owls and trees and spiders for some sign to tell me where to go, another soul like me to tell me what to do. The house breathes while the town is dark, but there is no one here to answer me.

3

WHEN MAGGIE WAS EIGHT YEARS OLD, A DRUNK DRIVER HIT THEIR FAMILY CAR while they were on their way home from ice cream, and Maggie—who'd just unclipped her seat belt to pull on her jacket because the ice cream had made her cold—went flying between the two front seats and hit the dashboard headfirst.

The doctor at the ER said she was made of rubber, because she didn't have a scratch on her. But for Maggie it was the first time she'd ever realized—or at least *really believed*—that she was breakable.

Sometimes she wondered if the accident hadn't happened would she have turned out differently, a little more reckless like her friends: Jacie, for instance, seemed to think she could never get hurt and that adulthood would never arrive. But Maggie thought of the future all the time. And for college, life, all the stuff coming her way in that future—she needed money and a job.

Gill Creek—she noticed on her first trip into town that Monday on the job hunt—was a white town: white houses, white boats, white curbs, white outfits. It seemed to glow and reflect off the rippling, sparkling blue of Lake Michigan, dotted only with the changing colors of the leaves that lined the crisscrossed streets. Late-season tourists meandered up and down Main Street, strolling into poky, old-fashioned candy shops; pastel-washed clothing stores; fish boil restaurants (a local specialty her mom had threatened that they'd try); and cafés. Shops had started putting pumpkins by their doorways and hanging stalks of colored corn on their doors. It took about an hour for Maggie to size up the town—to measure its width and length and breadth against where she'd come from—and to know life was going to feel small here.

"Fudgies." That was what Elsa, the woman who stood before her, called them, but Maggie had to ask her to repeat herself. "Oh, that's a word for the tourists. For some reason, when people are on vacation, they love to buy fudge. You would *not believe* how much fudge Fudgies will eat any given summer."

A long day of walking had landed Maggie here. She'd filled out three applications—at two restaurants and one kite store—but it was pretty clear that the part-time jobs were drying up now that summer was ending: The clerks had taken her applications as if she were just another one of the day's hassles. She'd meandered all the way to the uglier end of Main Street—beyond the reach of the tourists' natural habitat—and arrived at a giant, yellow Help Wanted sign leaned against the side of a low, square, brick building. Only when she'd walked through the front door had she realized it was a sprawling antiques mall. Inside it smelled like dust and mothballs and stale cigarette smoke and old coffee. It was like something out of Charles Dickens: full of nooks and crannies and narrow walkways and pieces of furniture piled crookedly. A sign by the register announced that Elsa's Lost World Emporium did not take checks without proper ID. Maggie was just turning around to leave when Elsa had approached her and introduced herself. She was plump, moist-faced, probably in her late forties. She had shoulder-length, curly, dirty-blond hair. She wore bright orange-red lipstick and a sweep of sparkly, brown eye shadow with thick mascara.

"You here about the sign?" she asked. "You don't look like an antiques hound."

Maggie nodded uncertainly.

"What kind of grades do you get?" Elsa asked, looking her over distractedly and wiping the moistness from her forehead with one long, gray sleeve.

"As," Maggie responded. "I'm homeschooled by my dad now," she added, then speedily threw in, "but I'm self-disciplined." Was she actually trying to get this job?

"Have you had a job before?" Elsa fingered the golden crucifix around her neck.

Maggie nodded and shifted from foot to foot.

"Well, this one's pretty simple—just ringing up customers, keeping inventory, keeping up with the vendors and communicating about their stalls—but I need to know you're reliable. Are you reliable?" Maggie nodded. She wondered if anyone had ever said no.

Elsa looked into her eyes as if searching for something. "Yeah, I think you are." She reached out and shook her hand. "It's eight bucks an hour. You can work weekend mornings and some evenings if it's busy. Be here at nine a.m. Saturday. I keep a key hidden by the sidewalk at the side entrance, under the fifth rock from the door, in case you get here before me. I'm your boss."

Maggie shook her hand limply, taken aback that Elsa would entrust her with a hidden key so easily. Also she hadn't even said she wanted the job. And eight bucks was next to nothing . . . which wasn't surprising, considering it didn't exactly look like a lucrative place.

On the other hand, she needed *something*.

She walked outside in a daze. Making her way back down Main Street to where she was supposed to meet her dad, she reasoned with herself that she could always quit.

She met her dad in front of the hardware store—they'd split up to take care of their separate errands. He was looking at the big, grinning pumpkin behind the glass and sipping some coffee. "This town is so quaint, I almost can't take it," he said. "Someone *made* that papier-mâché pumpkin."

"Amazing," Maggie said drily. As they walked back toward the car, Maggie stopped suddenly in front of a boutique with a red-striped awning, struck by a dress in the window. It was a pale, sea-foam green dotted with tiny rust-colored airplanes. Maggie was mesmerized by it. It was the colors she loved: It was rare for them to be just right, but in this case, they were perfect.

"I want that so much, it hurts," she said to her dad.

Her dad leaned close, and she realized he was trying to read the price tag. She leaned in beside him. "Whoa," she said.

"The blue one's cheaper," he offered hopefully. Suddenly she felt guilty for mentioning it. Just to be polite, she looked closer at the blue one too. It *was* cheaper, but still too expensive for them, even despite its ugliness.

"Actually they're not that great," she said, covering. "I didn't realize it was airplanes; I thought it was birds. Never mind."

She started to walk away and her dad followed, but, glancing back, she could see the pain on his face. She wanted to kick herself.

The first time her mom had gotten laid off, Maggie hadn't realized how bad things were until she'd opened her birthday present and found a handmade rug that her mom had hooked together herself. "I bought it at Anthropologie," her mom had said, and she'd pretended to believe her.

She had to do better, she knew. She had to take care of her parents just like they'd always taken care of her.

Back home, though she was tired from walking, she got right into her running shoes. Just as she'd expected, the run soothed her. She turned at the silo again and thought that at least this—this running route—was perfect; she couldn't ask for a better one: beautiful, challenging enough but not too hilly, and the fresh air felt great in her lungs.

Turning back, she listened to her heartbeat and the crickets and the sound of her sneakers on the pavement and the distant sound of the hammering in the woods, getting closer and closer as she got back toward Pauline's. She passed the long driveway with the mailbox marked No Trespassing and, turning toward the property, could hear the hammering far back and to her left.

Thinking of what Pauline had said, she thought maybe she should go say hi. She hesitated, then veered off the path and into the pine trees. She found the source of the noise in the middle of a stand of four tall pines. It was like the setting from an old German fairy tale: a glade with a small, pine-needle-blanketed clearing; a slant of light; and in the middle of it all, an exquisite, miniature wooden house— skinny and pointed at the top, big enough to fit maybe four people inside if they stood shoulder to shoulder. The roof was missing a piece, and one wall was still open to the elements, and on that side a figure knelt, hammering.

He looked up just as Maggie came even with the last pine tree. He stood.

"You must be Maggie," he said. He didn't smile, but his face wasn't unfriendly.

"Hey." She wiped a hand on her sweatpants, catching her breath, and waved tiredly. "You're Pauline's Liam."

He squinted slightly, amused. "Yeah, that's me." Liam wasn't what she'd pictured. She'd been imagining someone who complemented Pauline—a handsome, strapping, well-dressed type—but Liam had a subtle, soft look about him: medium-framed, tall, he was dressed in a frayed gray T-shirt that had seen better days and worn jeans. He had shortish brown hair that fell a little over his blue eyes and pale skin that looked like it would blush easily—Maggie thought of it as British-boarding-school-boy skin. He squinted, his brows furrowed. "Welcome to our lonely little spit of land." In his hand he grasped an intricately carved piece of wood.

"Thanks. What's that?" she asked.

"Oh." Liam looked down at his hand and frowned thoughtfully. "It's nothing. It's the roof." He held it up. "What do you think?"

It was a decorative edge for the roof—covered in intricate carved curlicues. It looked Scandinavian, like the carved bow of an old Viking ship.

"You made that?" she asked.

"Yeah." Liam nodded.

"What is it?" she asked, gesturing to take in the whole scene. "A home for elves?"

Liam didn't seem to notice the joke. He laid down the wood and rubbed the tip of his thumbnail along his bottom lip thoughtfully. "It's a Finnish sauna. My dad taught me how to do it. It's for Pauline, because she's cold all winter."

Maggie figured a girl as tiny and birdlike as Pauline probably had the circulation of her nana.

"Do you mind if I look?" Maggie asked. Liam considered, then motioned for her to step up to the little building and look inside. There were two benches—one on either side— and a slatted crate in the back that looked like the place for the coals. Not that Maggie knew much about saunas, but she'd been in one at her mom's gym back home once.

"It's not . . . it's not perfect. I've never done one."

"How long did it take you?" Maggie asked.

Liam put his hands in his pockets. "All summer, pretty much."

What guy spent his whole summer alone in the woods building a sauna? Clearly one of few words. The silence stretched on between them. Maggie was used to chatty guys. The guys in her circle of friends back in Chicago had been loud, always trying to impress each other.

A moth flew across her sight. Liam's eyes followed it, then

turned back to her in a friendly, open gaze.

"I've been reading about moths," she said, to fill the silence.

"What have you read?"

Maggie shrugged. "They navigate by the light of the moon. They fling themselves into flames and electric lights because they think they're headed toward the moon's light."

"I guess they die in ecstasy then," Liam said. His eyes followed the moth, tracking it into the trees.

"What do you mean?" Maggie asked, confused.

"Well, they probably think they've finally reached the moon." Liam's mouth spread into a slow smile that put her more at ease.

"Yeah, I guess it's probably the pinnacle of their moth lives," she conceded.

"All seven days or so."

They lapsed into silence for a few more seconds, but it wasn't a bad silence. He was strange, definitely. But she didn't necessarily mind strange.

"How long have you and Pauline been together?"

"Since we were five. We met"—Liam pointed the stick of wood in his hands toward Water Street—"there, in the middle of the street. We both hid behind our dads. I was eating baby carrots."

"How do you remember something that far back?" Maggie asked, laughing.

Liam rubbed the back of his neck, reddening slightly. "It's

Pauline. I have a weirdly long memory when it comes to her. Wanna sit?"

They sank onto a log, and Liam picked up his piece of wood again and began sanding it. Maggie looked around at the trees and listened to the birds. It was one of the quietest conversations of her life, but she felt, somehow, completely comfortable, sitting there with this guy she'd just met, not saying anything.

Finally Liam looked over at her. "I'm sorry, I'm not much of a talker. Pauline says I should learn to talk about stuff that doesn't matter, because people love that."

"People do love that," Maggie said, amused.

She studied his profile while he worked on the sanding, reflecting that he wasn't really her type, physically. She could see how he might be appealing to Pauline though, or to other girls in general. He was gently handsome, his eyes the softest thing about him, but the effort he'd put into the sauna hinted at something more rugged than first met the eye. His hands looked rough and scraped up from building. He was clearly used to physical work. "I hear Pauline roped you into canoeing already," he said, to the wood he was sanding vigorously.

"I didn't . . ." Maggie trailed off; she didn't know what to say. More than not knowing how to swim, she hated not seeing what was underneath her in the water.

Liam kept his eyes on his work. "You can try to resist her, but it won't work; Pauline gets what she wants. Take it from one who knows."

"I'm already beginning to get that feeling." Maggie lifted her eyebrows in the direction of the sauna, and then they both looked in the direction of Pauline's house—just a distant blob of white peeking through the trees.

"She's decided you're her new, good friend." He flashed her a quick smile as his eyes caught hers, one that disappeared just as quickly.

They sat in silence for a while longer. Another moth landed on a stump a couple of feet away.

"I think this guy hatched right over there."

Maggie looked at him. "You know all the moths?" she teased. "Are you some kind of moth whisperer?"

"He has a cocoon on that tree." He pointed, then seemed to notice the look on her face. "I'm not Old Man Nature or anything. It's just when you work out here all day, it's hard not to notice what the other animals are doing."

Liam put down his work again and leaned back, stretching. It was almost dusk.

"Well." Maggie stood. "I'm sure you're trying to get some stuff done before dark. . . ."

Liam didn't argue politely like she'd expected him to. He just held up a hand and waved to her.

"Nice to meet you," he said.

She turned and started away.

"Maggie," he called behind her suddenly, and she turned. "It's not a bad place. It's pretty nice. You'll like it."

"Um. Thanks."

She lifted her hand in the air in a wave and then turned and jogged back toward the main road.

There was something about Liam—his strangeness, his quietness, his alertness to things like cocoons—that made Maggie feel lighter as she jogged down the remainder of Water Street. It wasn't every day that she met someone who surprised her—most people were surprisingly *unsurprising*. And now she'd met two.

The sun was just sinking under the horizon as she reached her property—it glinted like the top of a gold coin and then disappeared behind the water. She could hear her dad out in the back field mowing down the tall grass, but here on this side, the lawn was still thick and overgrown and full of grasshoppers scattering and collecting and scattering again. In the fading yellow light, the metal roof of her house glinted, and Maggie lifted her face to the breeze coming off the water and making the low trees sway. She finally trudged through the grass to the lakeshore, then dipped a finger in the cold water.

She looked out at the lake and tried to make out which dots in the distance were the islands she'd read about, and where all the ships might have gone down. Someone had made a campfire on one of the beaches protruding along the shore to the north, and the smell of the smoke wafted to her on the breeze. The sound of some people laughing far away echoed across the water, and Maggie remembered reading that water was a great conductor of sound. She felt relaxed and peaceful in a way she didn't remember feeling much in the city, and she tried to take a moment to appreciate it.

Maggie didn't think she believed in God or astrology like Jacie back home did or even interpreting her dreams—nothing that she couldn't touch and feel and see. But she found herself saying a prayer; for what, she wasn't quite sure: to move back to Chicago, to be happy here, to be safe from the big things she couldn't anticipate. She said a prayer for the dead girl in Whitefish Harbor, just because she happened to think of her. She found herself longing for something that she couldn't put her finger on.

And then, because a fall coolness had crept into the air after the sun had dipped, she wrapped her hands around her arms and shivered and turned back across the grass.

4

MAGGIE KNOCKED ON PAULINE'S DOOR SUNDAY AFTERNOON, AFTER QUICKLY changing out of the clothes she'd worn to work. The Emporium was already underwhelming and it was only day two; the morning had seemed to last forever.

The temperature had dropped a little; she rubbed her fingers and tucked her hands into her pockets as she stared across the browning field at the changing leaves until Pauline opened the door in her pajamas, clutching a big mug of hot tea. Her face lit up. "You came."

Inside, the house was immaculate: marble floors, artsy rugs, sculptures, and couches that looked so soft you could sink into them and never come out. The AC was on full blast despite the cool weather. It all seemed hermetically sealed.

They crossed a vast living room toward a set of stairs that curled up to the second floor.

Reaching the bottom of the stairs, Maggie noticed that someone was on one of the couches and realized it must be Pauline's mom.

Mrs. Boden sat in front of the TV with a magazine. She looked up and smiled politely at Maggie.

"This is Maggie from next door," Pauline said. "We're going canoeing."

"Hi, Maggie," she said distantly. "Nice to meet you. I'm sorry I haven't been over to meet your parents yet." She was pretty in a mom way—blond with catlike brown eyes—and she looked younger than Maggie's mom. She had perfectly straight posture, and her clothes—dark pants and a cardigan over a tank top—were immaculate, as if she'd ironed them. Maggie wouldn't have picked her out as Pauline's mom in a million years. "How are you liking it here so far?"

"It's nice," Maggie said.

"That's great." She looked at Pauline. "Anyone else going?"

"Liam," Pauline said, giving Maggie a beleaguered glance.

"Huh," was all her mom said.

Maggie followed Pauline up the carpeted stairs to the upstairs hallway and they turned right.

Pauline's room was, in contrast to the rest of the house, chaotic—her clothes were in an enormous pile in the middle of the room, and her walls were covered in magazine clippings of flowers and hummingbirds and abstract art, taped messily here and there, with no apparent design or reason. Little knickknacks—a papier-mâché heart like a child might have made; a violin-shaped music box; a little, white ceramic ghost—were scattered and bunched on her dresser along with expensive perfume bottles, all missing their tops. Pauline pulled pants and shirts out of the clothes pile indecisively (Maggie noticed some designer labels), finally settling on a wrinkled, blue sweater and jeans. She changed right in front of Maggie.

"Your mom seems really different from you," Maggie said.

Pauline buttoned her jeans with her tongue between her lips. "Yeah. She's . . ." Pauline glanced briefly in the mirror and tucked her long, messy dark hair behind her ears. "She's really *polite*."

She led Maggie back downstairs and across the living room, where she kissed her mom on the cheek. "Love you, Mommy." Mrs. Boden patted her hand and said she loved her too. Pauline grabbed a grocery sack off the kitchen counter and then led Maggie out of the house.

Liam was waiting for them at the water's edge.

The girls loaded themselves into the canoe, Maggie pulling on one of the two life jackets as she sat down. Liam launched them and then climbed in after them. While he rowed them away from the shore, Pauline dug into the sack and pulled out a bag of Cheetos. In a moment she had them open and was stuffing them into her mouth and leaning over the edge of the boat to see if she could spot any fish.

"Don't tip us, woman," Liam called to Pauline, who was half dangling a foot over the side. Maggie glanced over her shoulder at him, and he grinned. He was more animated around Pauline. "She's dunked me more times than I can count. It's like she does it on purpose."

Maggie put her dark hair in a clip and then double-checked that her life jacket was on tight enough. It was shaping up to be a dazzling, cool fall day. The sky was pure blue, and the sunlight glinted off the water. Pauline righted herself and turned to look at them. "My dad and I used to canoe all the time when I was little."

"Not anymore?" Maggie asked.

Pauline paused a moment, tapping her heels against the side of the boat, sitting on her hands, and looking out at the island to their left. "Well, he died." She said it lightly, as if trying not to land too hard on the words. "He was a fisherman who married into the *great tea fortune*," she went on, "but he was just your average town guy. He was from Gill Creek. He was really funny; he made my mom laugh at everything, even herself. She really isn't a laugher anymore, but he could crack her up. I think that's why she married him, even when the rest of her family thought she was crazy. He *loved* Liam."

Maggie wasn't sure whether she was supposed to ask anything or not.

Pauline gazed around the sides of the boat, getting her bearings. "It didn't happen far from here. He had a heart attack. He and some friends were out here on a fishing boat. It was one of those freak things."

Chills ran up and down Maggie's arms.

"It happened when I was eleven." Pauline shrugged. "And that was it."

"Wow, I'm so sorry," Maggie muttered.

"It seems like a long time ago." Pauline's eyes narrowed, and she wiped slowly at the hair that was flapping against her face. "I always think of it out here. Well, I mean it's hard to forget your dad's dead, so I think of it a lot, but especially out on the lake. My mom never comes out on the water because of it. But I don't want to miss something just because . . . things went wrong. Life is short." She shrugged again, then clasped her hands together. "That's the biggest thing I learned from my dad."

Pauline pointed, and Maggie saw, to her surprise, that they'd floated out past a tip of land, and they had a perfect view of downtown, tiny in the distance.

"I didn't know you could see town from all the way out here," she said.

"Oh yeah, definitely. It's not as far as it seems when you drive. Actually people used to walk across the ice to town, back in the old days," Pauline said. "When it got cold enough to freeze solid, or I guess when they got desperate enough. Lots of history around here, you'll see. Lots of weird, cultural tidbits."

Maggie gazed at the little town in the distance, wondering if she could see the roof of the Emporium.

"Like, have you heard about Pesta?" Pauline asked suddenly.

Maggie shook her head. "Who?"

Pauline glanced at Liam, and Maggie looked at him over her shoulder. He rolled his eyes good-naturedly. "It's a Norwegian myth," she went on. "You know, a lot of Scandinavian people settled up here."

Maggie nodded—it'd been hard *not* to notice on their drive in: the euro-themed chalets; names on the mailboxes like Haugen and Bjornsson; the Scandinavian-themed restaurants (one with mountain goats on the roof); the Viking-themed cafés scattered among old fireworks stands, pickle shops, bakeries, everything that seemed to speak of summer tourism.

"She's a dead old lady," Pauline went on. "She's basically the lady grim reaper. She wanders the rocky shores and collects the souls of the dead and haunts the houses, waiting. If you look out your window and see her ambling along the shore toward your house, you're . . . well . . ." She turned two thumbs down.

"Well, thanks for telling me," Maggie said. "I'll never sleep again."

Pauline let out a scratchy "ha."

For the rest of the ride they explained to her about Gill Creek, describing the two main groups: the retirees and the people who'd been born here. They told her where the tourists went (the restaurants downtown) and where the locals went (bonfires on the beach, a greasy spoon called Isla's, a place called the Coffee Moose). They told her about Washington Island—which, Pauline said, was so stark and beautiful it could be Iceland—and, beyond it, deserted Rock Island. They promised to take her there on the ferry sometime.

Pauline went to a private school in Sturgeon Bay, she explained, and Liam had graduated (he was almost eighteen) and was doing part-time jobs with a catering company to help his dad pay the bills, until he figured out what to do next. All this time Pauline lay, squinting her face up to the sun, legs draped against Liam carelessly, like a little kid. She looked to Maggie, at that moment, so pretty and long-limbed and perfect—her tangled, glossy hair sweeping down behind her over the side of the canoe.

Eventually Liam turned the boat and started rowing toward a long, deserted beach covered in smooth pebbles. They climbed off the boat, and Pauline started building a little picnic for them: a blanket, cheese, Pepsi, snacks. They lounged back on the blanket and looked out at the water.

It felt, to Maggie, like they'd paddled to the edge of the earth.

"Let's swim," Pauline said, standing.

Maggie shook her head. "I don't swim."

Pauline was already pulling off her shirt—stripping down to her pale-pink underwear. There was a long, skinny scar down the side of her back, which only seemed to emphasize her beauty. Pauline held up an ugly, orange life jacket. "Sorry,

I forgot. We could just wade in. Come on."

"No thanks," Maggie said, shaking her head. "Anyway, it's too cold."

"The lake keeps the heat for a while."

Liam snorted behind her.

Maggie shook her head. "I didn't bring a suit anyway." There was no way she'd strip to her undies in front of Liam, and her curves weren't as easy to miss as Pauline's were. But really, it was the water itself—dark and deep—that she was resisting.

"Well, just wade in in your clothes." Pauline waved her forward. "You'll dry off in the sun."

Maggie sighed, thinking she could stay in the shallows at least. She stood and rolled up her pants above her knees and smoothed back her hair. She waded out into the cold water to Pauline's side, getting used to the temperature bit by bit, letting just the bottoms of her pants get wet. Pauline reached out to hold her hand, and Maggie awkwardly let her tug her along. Liam stayed on the shore, building a rock pile.

The water was bracing, but the cold was kind of thrilling. Pauline let go, crouched underwater, and then stood, spitting out a stream of water like a fountain and seeming not to notice her underwear was practically see-through.

"So how long have you guys been together?" Maggie asked. "Liam said you met when you were little."

"Me and Liam?" Pauline's eyes widened and she pursed her lips thoughtfully, pasting her wet hair back into a Mohawk with her hands. "Oh, we're not together. People think that sometimes, but . . . nooo. We're friends."

"Oh, I thought . . ."

"Yeah, everybody thinks that. My mom would be pretty upset if I dated Liam," Pauline said, low, as Maggie came abreast of her. "She keeps threatening to send me to Milwaukee to live with my aunt, and I'm pretty sure it's because of him; she says we spend too much time together."

Maggie glanced back at Liam, who seemed to be staring with extra focus at his rocks.

"What does she have against him?" Maggie asked.

Pauline thought. "Well, his dad's pretty weird. You'll see. He's really antisocial; he has an auto shop, but he barely talks to the customers. But on the other hand he's this outspoken atheist. He's got a Russian accent. I guess he moved to the States a few years before Liam was born, and then Liam's mom moved back. Anyway, people talk about him." Pauline reflected, then snorted. "The best thing is he's got this VW Bus painted with all these atheist slogans, and he drives back and forth past the New Community church for twelve-o'clock mass, every Sunday. It's hilarious. But I guess the downside is people think he's literally crazy."

Pauline began to wade back toward shore, but Maggie stayed behind for a few moments. She saw that, as Pauline climbed out of the water, Liam's eyes darted up to her and lingered, before he turned back to the ground. Just as Maggie had suspected, he blushed easily, pink creeping up his cheeks. Pauline, apparently oblivious, wrapped her shirt around herself like it was a small towel and jumped up and down to warm herself. Liam was only a year older, but he gave off the feeling of being much older than Pauline. It was like they'd grown up beside each other but at different speeds. For one, he couldn't seem to make his eyes stay away from her, while Pauline seemed to have the lack of modesty and self-consciousness of a child.

For a split second, Maggie wished someone would look at *her* like that. She'd gotten the nickname Saint Margaret back in Chicago because she'd barely even kissed anyone. But Maggie was no saint—it was just that her friends pretended sex wasn't complicated. Maggie wasn't ever going to walk into anything with her eyes closed, even if all her friends were jumping in with both feet. Still, she wanted things other people wanted. She just *carefully* wanted them.

They packed up and canoed home just as the sun was starting to set. The air was getting cooler each night, and goose bumps prickled along Maggie's arms and legs. Liam must have noticed, because he threw her the flannel shirt that was balled up in his lap. Once they were on dry land, they put the canoe in the boathouse. "Hey, I wanna show you guys something," Liam said, leading them up into the yard.

Pauline glanced back at them. "Can't. My mom and I have a date to watch *Friday Night Lights* on Netflix." She sighed. "I wish she'd go on a real date and let me off the hook." She threw her arms around Maggie and then Liam and jogged up to her back deck. She waved over her shoulder before she disappeared into the big, white house.

"Well, I can still show *you*," Liam said, obviously disappointed but putting on a kind face. Maggie was wet and cold, but she was curious. They made a diagonal into the woods and toward the water, walking past Liam's property and farther on. They seemed to be turning away from the water when the trees opened up and they were looking at a little inlet, almost as round as a pond, surrounded by trees and bathed in the early moonlight. What startled her were the brown-and-white-speckled shapes. There had to be about a hundred of them, swirling around the water and perched on the banks. Canada geese. Many of them sleeping, some of them preening themselves or each other.

"They rest here on their way south from Canada," Liam said. "Every year. Same time."

A flock of geese wasn't something Maggie would have paid attention to back home. But there was something magical about the sight of their white tail feathers rustling in the twilight. It seemed weird to her that, all the years she'd lived in the city, every fall the geese had been here—not so far away—inhabiting a whole different, quieter world. She and Liam hunkered back against an old tree stump, and the few geese that had seemed suspicious began to settle in. A couple of them even swam up to the edge, then waddled out of the water, shaking their feathers. They came right up to Liam.

"Sorry, guys, nothing for you this time." He reached out

his hand slowly and gently, and one of the geese examined his empty palm.

"I usually bring food. A lot of them are the same ones from other years—they always come back to the same spot. So they know me." He wriggled his fingers and turned his palm downward, and the goose lost interest and waddled away. "Pauline loves them, but she never remembers that they're coming back, so I usually can surprise her. Actually she tried to get me to catch her a goose once, when we were ten. It didn't go very well. I ended up in the lake."

"Do you do whatever Pauline asks you?" Maggie asked, teasing, a little touched by his devotion. It seemed old-fashioned—not like the way modern boys were.

Liam frowned thoughtfully. "I can't help it. My dad taught me that's what guys are supposed to do. If a girl wants something, you're supposed to do whatever you can to give it to her. Not that it really worked out for him." He sat back and looked up at a cloud passing over the new moon; it was almost a pale pink against the darkening sky. "You want that cloud?"

Maggie laughed. "Yes, please. I've had my eye on it for quite some time."

Liam began drawing numbers on his palm with his finger, brows knitting together. "Just calculating the angle and velocity I need to shoot it out of the sky." Maggie laughed, and two geese lifted off the lake and landed a few feet farther away. Liam looked toward the water again and began counting to himself in a whisper—counting out the number of geese. For some reason she couldn't explain, Maggie thought about touching the back of his neck, how warm it would feel in the cold air.

"I'd better get home," she said, standing and brushing off her legs. "My parents will wonder where I am."

Without a word, Liam nodded and led her back through the woods, even though darkness had fallen almost completely. He knew the way by heart, taking turns where she could see only shadows ahead. At the edge of the lawn, Maggie handed him his shirt. "Good night. Thanks for the geese."

Maggie was halfway across the kitchen when her mom appeared in the archway, a look of relief on her face.

"Oh, I'm glad you're home, Mags. I've been worried," she said. Then she turned back the way she'd come. "We're just watching the news. How was your day?"

Maggie followed her in through the glass doors to the parlor, where her parents had set up their small, ancient TV. "Why were you worried?" she said.

Her eyes followed her mom's to the television screen, which showed a high school graduation photo of a girl holding a rose. A news announcer was describing her as bright and beautiful and promising. *Second girl missing*, it said at the bottom of the screen.

"She went hiking on the dunes and didn't come back," her mom said. "You always think about your own kids when something like this happens."

Maggie watched, bothered. Why did reporters always mention how the dead or missing girls looked? As if it mattered. Did they say missing guys were handsome? *The young, handsome missing boy . . .*

"How was canoeing?" her mom asked. "Does Pauline have friend potential? What's she like?"

Maggie thought. "Yeah, I guess so. She's"—she tried to think of the best word to describe Pauline—"really pretty." Then thought what a hypocrite she was.

Her dad cocked his eyebrows at her wryly. "Is that good or bad?"

Maggie stuck her thumbnail in her mouth, absently. "Both, probably. For her."

"Well, you're the best-looking girl I know."

"You're genetically predisposed to say that."

"Doesn't mean it's not true."

That evening, after getting the chill out of her bones with a long, hot bath, Maggie sat on the back porch, bundled in a blanket, with a European history textbook on her lap, staring at the lake. Instead of thinking about the day on the water, she wondered if the missing girl might be out there somewhere, lost in the watery dark.

To Maggie and Pauline and Liam, Lake Michigan must look as pristine as a blank sheet of paper. But I've had a deeper view.

I've been to the bottom of the lake I can't remember how many times, and here's what I've seen: old cars that once tried to cross the ice in winter and fell through; houses that have disintegrated along the water's edge; things that people have thrown in, in the hopes they'd never be seen again: diaries, tires, refrigerators, even photos. If you're a wisp like me, you can sink down underwater and see for yourself what's been lost to the world above: skeletons trapped in boats, the rusted windows and doors of iron trawlers half sunk in sand. I don't know where the ghosts that belong to these skeletons have gone. They've left only their bones. I've been looking for other spirits all along the shore, wanting to ask my questions, but it seems I'm the only one.

In the cellar, where I sleep, there's one thing that frightens me, and I'd like to ask about that too—maybe most of all. It's a pinprick of light coming from the floor by the far right wall. It's impossible for that to be, but there it is.

I won't go near it. Something deep down tells me it

spells the end of me. I'm not ready.

And I think something is coming for one of these girls, or both.

I think I'm here to save them.

5

THE BEAUTIFUL, PROMISING GRADUATE WAS FOUND THE FOLLOWING SATURDAY, floating by the main dock in Ephraim, arms spread out like she was trying to fly away. As with the first girl who'd died, there wasn't a mark on her to indicate a struggle. The coroner ruled it death by drowning. Everyone at Elsa's Lost World Emporium was talking about it when Maggie walked in on Sunday morning.

The temperature had dropped drastically overnight, and after hurrying across the parking lot without her coat, Maggie welcomed the warm air of the Emporium despite the smell of dust and burned coffee. Elsa had the *Gill Creek Crier* spread out across the front counter and refused to look up from it even when a customer stood waiting for her.

"It's antiques," she said unapologetically, after Maggie slid in beside her and watched her slowly ring up the woman, "it's not brain surgery. People can wait."

Maggie leaned against the counter and read over her shoulder. Elsa poured her a cup of coffee. "It's getting cold out," Maggie said.

"A fisherman found her while he was headed back in. Her parents lost it." Elsa pointed to the article as if Maggie needed proof that parents would "lose it" in that situation, then fanned her face with her hand, getting flustered. "It's too much of a coincidence—two girls in three weeks. Someone killed those girls." Elsa shook her head. "Why them? Is it because they were young, or are older women a target too?" She shook her head again, harder, this time clicking her tongue. "Things like this don't happen here," she sighed. It seemed to Maggie that Elsa was enjoying herself a tiny bit. Maggie tried to change the subject, but Elsa kept circling back to it: the girl, her straight As, how pretty she was. "I'm not a good person in situations like this," Elsa went on. "I'm the first person to get hysterical. I drove all the way to Target this morning to buy pepper spray."

"You know, you just have to think of the statistics," Maggie offered. "Statistically it's highly unlikely anything will happen to you." She didn't like to linger over the terrible things in the news.

"Do you know some guy drove to Nashville from

California because he wanted to capture Taylor Swift and keep her in his basement?" Elsa went on, as if she hadn't heard her. "There are crazy people out there." Elsa had a pile of *People* magazines beside the cash register to prove it, and Maggie was beginning to think that Elsa saw Taylor Swift, and possibly Lindsay Lohan too, as part of her extended family. "Some crazier than others." Elsa's eyes lifted to follow Gerald as he walked past carrying the horn of an old gramophone.

Two weeks in, Maggie was already getting used to the Emporium's rhythms and its weird smells and quirky vendors. Gerald had a stall near the back of the store, where he sold mostly gramophones, old radios, and old record players, one of which was usually going at any time. He always played oldies, and Maggie liked to hear the music drifting from the back of the store, usually Billie Holiday or Etta James. He *did* look crazy—he had stark-white hair, a bony face, and big, protruding, piercing, blue eyes that reminded her of an eagle. Maggie sometimes caught him eyeballing her. Now, with Elsa staring him down, he apparently didn't have the nerve to gawk and kept walking to the back of the store.

Elsa leaned her elbow down on the counter and nodded toward Maggie conspiratorially. "It's him. I'll bet you. We're working with a . . ." And then Elsa mouthed the word *psychopath*.

"Just because he looks weird doesn't mean he's a killer," Maggie said. "Older guys who like to stare at teenage girls aren't that rare, unfortunately."

Elsa folded her arms, gazing down the aisle, then reached a finger up to dab at the corner of her lipstick. "Well, it doesn't mean he isn't."

At that moment a sound drifted to them from the back of the store. He'd put another record on the gramophone, something old and jazzy and instrumental.

Elsa raised her eyebrows. "You tell me listening to old, scratchy records isn't something a psychopath does."

"A psychopath or a music lover," Maggie said sardonically.

Elsa smirked, rolled her magazine, and swatted Maggie with it. "Next time I'll hire a B student. You're a smart aleck." They both glanced up to see a girl coming toward them from the opposite direction. "Oh, here she comes," Elsa muttered, and moved to the farthest edge of the counter with her newspaper.

Hairica was what Elsa had christened her, though her real name was Erica. About Maggie's age, she occasionally worked in the shop covering for her mom. Their booth had the ugliest stuff in the Emporium: frilly, lace napkins and gaudy, overdecorated lamps. "Stuff only your dead great-grandmother would love," as Elsa said. Elsa, who happened to be Erica's next-door neighbor, had given her the nickname Hairica because she was unusually hairy: She had long hair down to her waist, a low hairline on her forehead, hairy temples, and very downy hair along her cheeks and chin. The first time Elsa had used the name to Maggie, Maggie had frowned hard at her to avoid laughing. She tried not to encourage Elsa's snarkiness, but it wasn't easy.

Now Maggie smiled kindly at Hairica as she approached the desk with a bright green imitation Louis XIV lamp, painted with bewigged people frolicking on a lawn.

"Can you put this in the ledger and ring it up?" Hairica asked, shyly glancing up at Maggie. "I just sold it." Maggie goggled at the price: $365.

Maggie wrote it all down in the proper columns. "That's . . . nice," she said.

"No, it isn't," Hairica said. A small, shy smile grew on her lips.

"Okay, it's hideous," Maggie admitted. Hairica laughed. Maggie opened her mouth to say something more, but Hairica blushed, turned, and walked back to her booth.

"Do you know Pauline and Liam, out on Water Street?" Maggie asked, turning to Elsa.

Elsa nodded. "I know everyone."

"They're my neighbors. They took me canoeing."

Elsa nodded, seemed to try to hold her tongue, but of course she didn't manage to succeed.

"I wouldn't put too many eggs in that basket if I were you."

"What do you mean?"

"Liam and his dad are weirdos. They make me nervous; at least the dad does. And the Bodens, they're just . . . into the Bodens." Maggie took this in, not knowing quite what to make of it. "You know pretty girls like that, with all that money. They just get used to everything revolving around them. Her mom's the same way. Self-absorbed. They think they're entitled to everything."

Maggie guessed so, but to her it seemed like the opposite. It seemed to her that Pauline was on the outermost edge of things.

But in a moment Elsa had moved on to talking about Matt Damon. In her eyes, Matt Damon could do no wrong.

After her shift Maggie spent the afternoon at the Coffee Moose, trying to make a dent in *Moby Dick*. That night, as she drove home, she saw that all the lights were on at the Boden house, and the sounds of a large party drifted out through the windows.

She felt a pang that she hadn't been invited, but she guessed she didn't know Pauline that well. Or maybe Elsa was right; maybe Pauline only wanted to hang out with her when she was bored. She was ruminating on this thought as she walked inside to find her parents poring over a box of financial records on the living room floor, doing their budget.

The house was coming along; that week her mom had spent her nights staining the floors on the first level so that they didn't look so scratchy and decrepit anymore. Maggie popped some clothes in the hamper. She read in the living room until after her parents had gone to bed.

Upstairs her room was stuffy; she could almost see the heat puffing out of the old radiator. She cracked open the window to let in the cold air, then stood and shivered and looked up at the stars, which seemed to get brighter every night as the weather got colder.

She noticed some movement in the grass between the two houses.

It was Pauline, standing in the moonlight. She was perched on a fallen tree that was propped at a sharp angle against another tree, walking up and down the incline with her arms spread wide to balance herself, wearing a knit hat and no jacket. She was so high that if she fell, she could have easily broken something, and Maggie sucked in her breath. Pauline happened to look up at Maggie's window at that moment and waved wildly, going off balance slightly before righting herself. Maggie closed her window, went downstairs, and walked outside and across the grass in her socks, the cold seeping into the soles of her feet.

"Are you practicing your balance-beam routine?"

Pauline didn't falter. "Oh yeah. I've been working on my dismount." She looked down, let her arms drop, sighed, then descended onto the grass. "I hate parties."

"Why?"

"Everyone wants to talk to me."

"That sounds terrible," Maggie said sarcastically. "You're, like, the opposite of a wallflower."

Pauline smirked. "I'm serious. I hate it. It makes me want to scream."

Maggie could picture it, how Pauline would draw people to her in a room, not just because of how she looked but because of her vibrating, infectious energy.

"Why does everyone talk about stuff that they only pretend to be interested in?"

"I don't know. It's just the way people are." Maggie shivered and wrapped her arms tightly around herself, shaking her legs to keep her feet warm.

"My mom's that way. But I think it's just because she's not that happy. Because she misses my dad. I won't be that way." Pauline sighed, a thin trail of white steam rising from her mouth, then studied her. "I wish I were more like you. You seem so calm."

Maggie shook her head. "I'm not calm, I'm just . . . *hesitant*. It's, like, I always think pretty soon my life will be this *great story*, as soon as it *starts*."

Pauline put one foot in front of the other, staring at her toes. "I can't picture that at all for me. You never know when you'll . . ." She stuck out her tongue to pretend she was dead. "I can't picture staying in Door County, and I also can't picture leaving. I can't picture the future." She grinned slyly. "Do you think that means I'll die young?"

"Probably."

Pauline laughed her scraping laugh that practically hurt the ears and climbed back onto the felled tree. "Maybe this is the way I go. On the dismount."

There was the squeak of a door opening onto Pauline's back deck and the sound of chattering and dishes and glasses clinking inside. And then Mrs. Boden's voice, calling to her.

Pauline stepped back down again, her shoulders slumping like a three-year-old's, her whole body curling over in disgust. "My mom always makes me hang around at these things because I'm her security blanket. Argh. Bye." She flung up her hand, wagged it, and started walking. "Oh wait, I'm sorry I didn't ask. Do you want to come over? It's really horrible."

Maggie suddenly felt guilty about what she'd thought earlier. She looked back toward her house, then back at Pauline, hugging herself tighter. "It sounds appealing, but no. I'm gonna read."

"Smarty-pants." Pauline turned and half slid, half walked across the lawn, as if she were on her way to the gallows.

Maggie couldn't concentrate on *Moby Dick*, and she couldn't sleep. She wandered the halls, padding along the smooth, wooden floors. The house felt huge and silent. Finally she crawled back into bed and stared at the ceiling. She didn't realize she'd fallen asleep until, around 4:00 a.m., she awoke to a woman's voice in the yard. At first she thought it was a real person, wailing. Then the noise separated itself into words. It wasn't wailing after all, but singing.

> *I saw my love walk down the aisle*
> *On her finger he placed a ring*
> *All I could do was cry*

It was a beautiful voice drifting up to the windows from the side porch. Maggie tiptoed downstairs and emerged wrapped in an afghan onto the wooden deck. A light came on behind her in the kitchen, and she was joined by her mother.

"That's Etta James," her mother said.

They both stood there staring at the instrument plugged into the porch outlet—a swirling, antique gramophone.

I drift into the gray morning air and follow a snow-flake down to the Larsen porch. The earth seems hushed as the first snow of the year falls on Maggie Larsen and her mom—just a light, thin covering, as if the winter were dipping in a toe. Their hair is soon sugar-dusted. I rise to the sound of Etta James.

I've started floating high above the peninsula to look for other ghosts like me on the land below, thinking they'll glow and give themselves away, because I remember that ghosts should glow. (Though maybe, I wonder, only to each other? Or not at all?) Besides the glare of electric lights, the peninsula is dark: large swaths of woods; long, dark shores.

Still, below, in the early dawn, something runs rampant through Gill Creek. It tips over garbage cans, taps against windows, breathes onto people's necks. The residents think it's animals, or the wind. But I think it's fear itself.

I return to Maggie, who's now alone on the porch. She feels it too, the icy cold down her neck, the sense of something threatening just beyond her reach. I try to imagine I'm her guardian angel—I try to send her strength, but she doesn't feel it.

She shivers in the cold, and the moment is gone.

6

MAGGIE WAS DRINKING COFFEE OVER HER TEXTBOOK AT THE GLASS KITCHEN table Tuesday—taking notes for a comparative-lit paper while her mom sat across from her, on the phone with her boss— when they heard a scratching at the door.

Maggie looked out the window, and no one was there. But when she placed her nose to the glass and looked down, she saw Abe sitting on the porch landing, tail *thwapp*ing against the slatted wood, a tiny slip of paper sticking out from under his collar. She opened the door and pulled the paper out of its spot.

Snow day, we're off. Didn't want to wake you. Gone to Liam's. Come over.

Maggie went to the fridge and rolled up a piece of ham for Abe, who chomped it and ran off. She checked with her mom, promising to come back in time to get a full day's school-work in, and then pulled on her boots and hat and coat and trudged across the fresh field, her tracks punctuating the white expanse behind her. Only about an inch of snow was on the ground, but it was enough to cover the whole field in a layer of white, making the features of the yard vanish. She breathed the cold air in deeply, and instead of taking the road she cut through the sparse woods, swinging by the sauna in the glade to check Liam's progress. (The roof was up, but the one wall was still missing, the empty space draped in a blue plastic tarp.)

Liam's house was a low, long, one-story wood cabin butt-ing right up near the edge of the lake and surrounded by thick trees. A thin thread of smoke was rising through the chim-ney into the air and filling the woods with a delicious, smoky smell. A cardinal crossed Maggie's path and she remembered her mom saying cardinals were the spirits of those we loved watching over us, though Maggie had never really lost any-one she loved. Maybe it was Pauline's dad.

The infamous VW Bus was parked in the driveway—it was old and rusty but painted a bright yellow. She could see the slogans "If Jesus is Inside me, I hope he likes Fajitas because that's what he's Getting!" and "Viva La Evolución!" painted across the side in purple. A vivid red devil was painted just behind the rearview mirror, hanging out with what looked like Bigfoot and the tooth fairy, and a slogan underneath that said "Scientists for Satan."

Liam answered the door in pajama pants and a button-down flannel shirt that hung half open, and Pauline lay draped on a thick rug in pajamas too, in front of the fire with a stick in her hand, roasting a marshmallow. Liam buttoned his shirt self-consciously while Maggie took in the house. It was full of handmade touches, like a cupola lined with copper above the living room and intricate woodwork around the windows.

"Where'd you get that?" Maggie asked, pointing to a model ship hanging from a corner of the ceiling. She'd never seen anything quite like it.

"I made it," Liam said sheepishly, looking upward. He stood with his hand on the couch.

"Liam can make everything. He built this house, pretty much," Pauline said, from the rug, lifting up her legs into the air so that she was shaped like an L.

Liam shrugged. "I helped. My dad and I remodeled it. It was kind of a shack before this."

They sat on the rug next to Pauline. "That must have taken forever," Maggie said.

"Four *long* years." Liam reached out his hand to receive a graham cracker from Pauline.

"S'mores for breakfast," Pauline said blissfully. Liam stoked the fire.

Maggie stared up at the ship, marveling at its tiny windows and little doors. How many hours had Liam spent working on it? There were other ships scattered about the house and carved wooden animals and rustic-looking furniture. Maggie loved everything about the place. It reminded her of where the elves lived in *The Lord of the Rings*.

"Come meet my dad," Liam said.

He led her through a cozy, wood-paneled hall toward the back of the house. Walking behind him, she smelled cedar and fire smoke and maybe Liam's soap. It was like she'd entered the Land of Men.

He turned right, and she followed him through a door and out into an attached garage. Its shelves were stacked with saws and carving tools. A man sat hunched at a worktable against the wall to the right and didn't look up to greet them.

"Dad. This is Maggie, our new neighbor."

Mr. Witte was still for a moment, as if absorbed in his task, and then he swiveled in his seat and looked up. "Hello, Maggie, our new neighbor," he said. He was bearded, and his eyes were blue and they twinkled. He looked like a Scandinavian villager in the 1800s. He wasn't what she'd been expecting.

"What are you working on?" she asked.

"Well, see for yourself." He had a dim hint of an accent.

Maggie edged closer. It was a model ship. He'd carefully and painstakingly painted the hull with black-and-yellow stripes. The whole thing was so tiny and intricate, it boggled Maggie's mind to think how it could have possibly been done.

"That's really nice, Mr. Witte."

Mr. Witte shrugged.

"Not something teenage girls are interested in."

"No, it's *really* interesting. It's really cool."

"What *are* you interested in?" he asked, sizing her up.

"Um, I like to read."

"Who's your favorite author?" he asked abruptly, cutting her off.

"Um." Maggie felt nervous, as if she were on a job interview. She looked at Liam, who widened his eyes at her apologetically. "I like the Brontës. Um, I'm reading *Moby Dick* right now."

"Pah. Melville was a plagiarist." He blew out through his lips and turned back to his work, unimpressed. "What about Tolstoy?"

Maggie shrugged. She hadn't read Tolstoy.

"Thomas Mann?"

She shook her head.

Mr. Witte sighed as if she'd disappointed him and resumed his work as if they weren't still in the room. Liam gave her a helpless look, as if to say, *That's about how it goes* and then led her back to the front room, where they sank onto the soft rug by Pauline. "I think he likes you," he said.

"Ha."

"No, seriously," Liam said, rubbing his jaw, embarrassed. "That's him being friendly. Sorry. He's grumpy and also convinced of his own superior intellect. But he's sweet underneath it all. He's a great dad."

Maggie told them about the gramophone she'd found on her porch, and about Gerald from the Emporium, and they were both equally horrified.

"I told my mom it was you guys. I don't want to worry her."

"You should tell her. You should have him arrested," Liam said.

"They can't arrest a guy for leaving a gramophone on your porch."

"Littering," Pauline offered hopefully.

"I don't even know if it was him. I called Elsa, and she said she'd have one of the guys at the Emporium talk to him. She won't talk to him herself, because she thinks he's the killer."

Pauline let out a loud groan. "Everybody thinks everybody is the killer. The lady at the 7-Eleven says it's that guy Sam from the Gill Creek Maritime Museum, because he has sinister eyebrows. I think it's Liam."

Liam stared into the fire. "I did it with s'more sticks."

"Anyway, the killings weren't anywhere near here. Sturgeon Bay is all the way down the peninsula. The whole thing will die down eventually," Pauline said.

"Well, the people of Door County can rest easy now that we have your expert opinion," Liam said flatly.

Pauline rolled her sock into a doughnut and threw it at him, and he caught it with one hand and gave her a look—they both looked angry and like they were going to laugh at the same time. There seemed to be this permanent electric tension between them—like a thread stretched from one to the other, pulling tight and loosening and pulling tight again.

"Do either of you want it?" They turned to look at her, confused. "The gramophone."

"I'd love it," Liam said.

"He'll take it apart, and it'll never go back together again. Like Humpty Dumpty. He disembowels everything to see how it works." Something vibrated, and Pauline pulled her cell phone out of her pocket. "You get a signal around here?" Maggie asked.

"Hardly ever. Sometimes around Liam's house. It's basically just for telling time. Bleh." She looked at the screen.

"What is it?"

"This guy from school, James Falk. He doesn't notice that I don't think he's as amazing as he does." Pauline tucked her phone away and turned back to the fire. She ignored Liam's dark look and held her hands out in front of her contentedly. "The fire's so nice and warm. Wouldn't you love to live somewhere that's warm all the time? I'd love to live in Austin, that's my dream. I'd love to be one of those singer-songwriters who perform in all the bars and wear sparkly pants."

"Are you moving there after you graduate?" Maggie asked.

Pauline wagged a hand in the air. "Eh. I don't know."

"Pauline doesn't believe in planning." Liam turned to Pauline with a chastising expression.

"But getting the things you want takes planning, if you

really want them," Maggie offered. This was her exact area of expertise.

"Yeah, but how can you really plan anything?" Pauline took another bite of s'more and spoke through her food. "Everything turns out totally different than what you plan."

Liam kneaded one hand in the other, clearly frustrated with Pauline. "Well, I doubt someone's going to come along and say, 'Hey, come sing at my bar in Austin, and by the way here's an apartment and a plane ticket.'"

"Are you so eager to get me to leave?" Pauline shot back, looking at him with a mock frown.

Liam laughed. "I just want you to have what you want."

"Well, *you're* not going anywhere," Pauline said teasingly.

He sat leaning his back against the couch and expertly searing the edges of his marshmallow, meticulously, perfectly even.

"*I* don't *mind* living up here. I like the cold. I like being near my dad. I could live in the north all my life." He snapped a graham cracker and laid the marshmallow on top. "There's stuff I'd like to *see* though."

"Like what?" Maggie asked.

Liam thought. "Well, up in Michigan there's this spring that's really deep, but it's crystal clear, forty feet to the bottom, like glass. It stays the exact same temperature all year, and you can see the springwater bubbling in through the sand on the bottom; the sand . . . *rolls*. My dad said it looks like the top of a volcano down there. And there are these big, silver trout that have lived in that tiny pond their entire lives. You're not allowed to go swimming there, but I'd like to."

"That's what you really want to see?" Pauline teased. "In this whole gigantic world? A trout pond a couple of hours away?"

Liam leaned back against the couch, unfazed. "I never said I was ambitious, Pauline." He raised his eyebrows at Maggie.

"What about you?" Pauline said. "Please tell me you have something more interesting planned than a trout stream."

Maggie shrugged. "Yeah, I have a lot planned. Northwestern. Then get a job in finance, most likely in downtown Chicago. I get nervous if I don't map things out ahead of time."

"Wow, you're such an adult," Pauline said wonderingly, then squinted as she studied Maggie.

"I get that a lot." Maggie was always the one her friends back home turned to for practical advice or Band-Aids or a nail file or hand sanitizer. (She kept supplies in her purse and backups in her backpack.) Jacie sometimes called her Grandma Mags.

"I actually can't picture that you were ever a kid," Pauline mused, resting her chin in her hands. Maggie was holding her half-eaten s'more unconsciously in one hand but paused as the comment hit home. It hurt a little. Quick as a fish, Liam darted his face to her hand and stole a bite. Then grinned at her. Maggie felt herself blushing.

"Let's go down to the Roadrunner and get pizza," Pauline said, suddenly standing and stretching, tall and skinny above them. "I'm starving." Maggie marveled at Pauline's appetite—she'd already had three double s'mores.

"Took the words out of my mouth." Liam stood, pulled his coat on off the couch, then picked up Pauline by her waist and moved her out of the doorway, pretending to need to get to the pizza first. Then he turned back and held the door open for them, suddenly gallant.

They piled into Pauline's car.

"Are you sure we can get through the snow?"

Pauline pinched Maggie's cheek and smirked. "City girl." The car started and stopped. "Sorry," Pauline said, leaning over the dash. "She's temperamental. Sometimes she goes. Sometimes she doesn't. My mom keeps trying to buy me a new car, but this one owns my heart."

She put the Subaru key on the dashboard, and Liam leaned forward from the passenger side and loosened the ignition by hitting it with the palm of his hand. He pulled it off, looking like a seasoned mechanic, fiddled a bit, then put the cover back on. This time, when Pauline tried the key, the car came to life.

"It's called finesse," Liam said. He fiddled with the knob, turned the heat on full blast, and kept fiddling with the vent so it would blow on her. Maggie heard something snap.

"Ugh." Pauline threw a look at Maggie in the rearview

mirror as they backed down the driveway. "He breaks everything."

As they ate—standing outside the shop, staring out at the bridge that crossed over the strait into mainland Wisconsin—Maggie thought how much she missed real Chicago pizza while Pauline held out her car key to Maggie, showing her that it was scorched and melted on one side.

"I threw it in our fireplace once, when I was really annoyed with the car." She tucked it into the pocket of her jeans, then looked up and over Maggie's shoulder. "Hey," she said, pointing through the glass wall of the pizza shop. "Look." Inside the store everyone—every single person—was staring up at the TV. "Let's go inside to hear better." They trickled in, rubbing their cheeks to warm them up, and listened and watched.

A third girl had been found in White Stone. She hadn't come home from school the day before, and they'd found her that morning in the water, about fifty yards offshore. The newscasters had started to use the word *serial*. An 8:00 p.m. curfew had been issued for the entire county for anyone under twenty-one. And the bridge between Gill Creek and the mainland would be put up tonight, in case the perpetrator was still on the peninsula and could be caught.

"Looks like you moved here just in time," Pauline said, "for the whole county to start shutting down around us."

* * *

That night, because Mrs. Boden was out at a town meeting, they watched movies on Pauline's giant TV. Pauline looked to be half asleep when she seemed to remember something and went into the kitchen, then came out again and handed Maggie a piece of paper.

"Here," she said.

Maggie stared at it. It was covered in pictures of Grumpy Cat, an angry blue-eyed cat from the internet.

"What is it?" she asked.

"Just a Grumpy Cat collage. I made it for you during study hall. I tried to capture all of his best expressions," she said sleepily, laying her head on the arm of the couch and stretching her legs onto Liam.

"Um, thanks?"

Pauline conked out halfway through the first movie.

"Does she always fall asleep so fast?" Maggie asked.

Liam nodded. "She falls asleep at the movie theater."

They turned back to the movie, then Liam went on, his voice low. "People think she's kind of this wild girl. But she's really just like a kid. She gets excited about everything, and then she crashes."

"Do you think we should leave?" Maggie whispered.

Liam rubbed his finger along his lip, studying Pauline as if trying to decide. Then he stood up. Without a word he crouched and lifted Pauline off the couch and put her over his shoulder. Maggie stood and watched him walk up the first couple of stairs, staying where she was, until Liam looked over his shoulder at her.

"Come on up."

Maggie followed him up the rest of the stairs and down the hall to Pauline's room. In the dim light from the hall, Liam walked over to the bed and laid Pauline down in it, first pulling back the covers and then bending to drape her on the bed. He pulled the blankets all the way back up to her chin, and Pauline's eyes fluttered for a moment and then closed again. She looked peaceful and, like Liam had said, kidlike. Liam touched his hand to her hair and kissed her on the forehead, and Maggie felt her heart beat faster, as if she were seeing something she shouldn't. Finally she turned away and stared into the dark hall. There were pictures on the wall of Pauline and her mom and dad through the years. Her mom looked a lot less polished, in T-shirts and jeans, and a lot happier in the eyes. Her dad, apparently, was where Pauline had inherited her coloring and her high cheekbones.

Maggie felt Liam approaching her, and he put his arm on the door over her head.

"She likes to wake up in her bed. She says it makes her feel cozy. For all I know, she's pretending she's asleep just so I'd carry her," he said.

He hovered there with his arm over her, and Maggie took a couple of steps backward. Stiffly she turned and led the way downstairs.

* * *

That night she pulled out her pencils again to have another go at the mural idea, but she couldn't think of anything to sketch. She pulled out a book on rocks that she'd gotten for her geology lessons instead. She loved the book, because it had shown her you could crack dull, ordinary rocks open and find colors inside. She considered retrieving a hammer from her dad's toolbox in the basement and taking it outside in the moonlight to rock hunt.

Despite being tired, her body was wide-awake. She found herself thinking about Liam Witte, who was not her type. She thought about the habit he had of rubbing his lip with his thumb.

Jacie used to say that Maggie was waiting until everything lined up *just so* before she really decided to live her life. But nothing about life on the peninsula was just so. Maggie wondered if this was how the *real* part of life started, with everything going slightly tilted and making you feel like things were rising in you, the thought of Liam Witte's thumb moving in your mind like ripples and waves.

7

GILL CREEK REACTED TO THE DANGER IN ITS MIDST WITH FEAR BUT ALSO a slight bit of pride. The county had never been at the center of things before. Father Stone at Maggie's church—which her parents had started making her attend every Sunday afternoon after work—had more fire in his step and more passion at the pulpit. More people came to church, maybe because there was safety in numbers. Reporters rolled into town, and cops patrolled in the evenings—which came earlier as the days got colder—to scan the streets for suspicious individuals. Maggie's dad installed a home alarm, even though she reminded him that it wasn't like the guy was sneaking into people's houses and taking them out of their beds.

The tourists were completely gone by now, and in

downtown Gill Creek, the seasonal restaurants and shops—
the kite store, the Scandinavian dessert shop where the
waitresses dressed up as milkmaids—had shut their doors,
their windows dark and gloomy as Maggie passed them on
her way to work. But the quiet also gave the town a certain
warmth—in the year-round cafés, people gathered for eggs
and fifty-cent coffee and huddled against the world outside,
and others caught up on the mostly empty Main Street and
talked in low voices about their theories on the killer.

At the Emporium business slowed, but no one seemed to
mind. Elsa hadn't gone into the antiques business, Maggie realized, to make money but to socialize, catch up with the people
who came and went, and have something to do. She could
have retired, she revealed one day, because she'd inherited
some money that made her retirement comfortable. Maggie, it
seemed, was the only one who desperately needed the job. And
luckily Elsa kept the Emporium open rain or shine.

One weekend after the next, Maggie rang up one dusty
thing and then another and another: a chamber pot, a Victorian hairbrush set, a yellowed copy of *Huck Finn*: proof—she
figured—that Gill Creek's long-dead residents had once
pooped, combed their hair, and read books just like people
today. She watched for Gerald, who came in only sporadi-
cally, and who Elsa said had denied everything, pointing
out that he sold at least one gramophone every two weeks
and that anyone could have bought one and left it on Maggie's porch. Maggie knew he must keep a detailed inventory

beyond the store's price ledger, and she still planned to confront him herself, but she was waiting for a moment that felt right.

Meanwhile she got Elsa's life story and all the local gossip: She learned all of Elsa's sister's annoying habits, she learned that the woman who lived in the white house at the end of Banks Street was a hoarder, that Ed who owned the fish boil was cheating on his wife, and that fishing in the northern tip of the lake was bad this year and everyone was drinking more than usual. She also heard, once or twice, about Liam and Pauline. She heard Pauline liked to sunbathe naked and that Liam and his dad sometimes sacrificed animals. Elsa talked about all of them the way she talked about celebrities. Maggie sometimes had to just tune her out.

At times like this, she missed Chicago, its largeness and anonymity. On a dare at a sleepover when they were younger, Jacie had once made her walk through Andersonville Park in a gold leotard and sling-on fairy wings, and no one had even stared. Maggie had been mortified, but Jacie had always been like that—loving and funny in a biting way. She wasn't the kind of friend Maggie had seen in movies, who she felt like she could open up to about her deepest secrets. Jacie was the kind of friend who made you walk through Andersonville Park in a gold leotard and said she was trying to get you to lighten up, and who sometimes got jealous when you got more attention from guys than she did. But Maggie still missed her like crazy.

One afternoon as Gerald walked in, he came right past the desk without looking at her. Maggie watched him out of the corner of her eye as he passed. Studying him intently for the first time, she noticed that he limped just slightly.

"Elsa, is there something wrong with Gerald's legs?" she asked, after he'd disappeared down the aisle.

"Well, *leg*. He's only got one," Elsa said matter-of-factly.

Maggie turned and looked at her, leaning on her hands. "Elsa, you said you thought he was the killer."

"Well, he could be."

"Don't you think it'd be kind of hard to capture and drown girls when you're that age and you only have one leg?"

Elsa shrugged. "I dunno how psychopaths do what they do." She proceeded to pick up a true-crime novel she was reading. As if anyone was more of an expert on psychopaths than Elsa.

Maggie tried to picture Gerald lugging the gramophone onto her porch. It didn't seem so sinister now. At worst, he was a creepy old guy with a crush, that was all.

The first week of November, summer ducked its head back in for a few last, rare days. Almost every day that week, Maggie could see Pauline and Liam out the window playing baseball in the damp, brown field in the evenings, Pauline winding up like a spider in water, Liam sizing her up in his serious, observant way before throwing his pitch. Sometimes she went to watch, and sometimes she stayed inside and worked on her schoolwork: comparative world lit, European history, advanced calculus, and French III.

"Sweets, can you pot all the geraniums and move them into the cellar?" her mom said on her way out one morning. "I want to bring them in for the winter. I wasn't expecting that early snow, but I'm hoping they're okay." She crossed her fingers in the air. Maggie wondered why her mom had planted them when they were just going to have to bring them back in, but she guessed she'd just gotten carried away with having a yard for the first time and wanting to make it nice.

She walked out to the garden that afternoon and surveyed the property. All in all, they'd made some good progress. Her father had painted two sides of the house so far. The field was tamed, and the bushes had been neatly trimmed so that they no longer looked like they were swallowing the house. The porch had been sanded, with boards replaced in some places, and her mom had hung some yellow wind chimes. The mailbox was painted, and they had cleared a pleasant little pathway between some semi-well-shaped shrubs from the back door to the driveway. The house no longer looked derelict or unlived in. She would have upgraded it to "shabby but charming."

Her mom had laid out all the planters. Maggie began to fill them—pulling out the geraniums from under the roots and tucking them into the potting soil—then hauling them toward the cellar door.

She turned at the sound of footsteps on the grass and

found Liam standing there with a shovel.

"Pauline thought you guys might need some help. She saw your mom putting out the planters this morning."

"Oh." Maggie wiped the hair out of her eyes. "Thanks. I'm okay actually."

She didn't want to be alone with him. It made her feel prickly.

"Okay," he said, and hoisted the next planter—the same size as the ones she'd been wrestling for an hour—into his arms like it was a feather. He lifted a second planter in his left arm and walked in the direction of the cellar. Maggie sighed and lugged one behind him.

They worked for about half an hour, digging, filling, hauling, until sweat covered their bodies and dirt covered their arms, legs, calves, faces. Gnats kept hovering around their sweat. Finally Liam laid the last planter near the cellar door and sank down on the grass. Maggie knelt a couple of feet away.

"So what's in the cellar?" he said.

"Besides the washing machine and dryer, I actually don't know."

"You're not curious?"

Maggie shrugged.

He opened the cellar door, and the smell wafted out to them, the cool air on their faces.

"Smells like the old days," Liam said with a grin. He climbed in and then helped her down, and her feet landed with a *thud* on the cold ground. The room was low and tight—the ceiling just over their heads.

He'd been joking, but it did smell like the past—like dust and things that people didn't use anymore: old oils, old metal, old leather, and air, Maggie imagined, that people had last breathed in the fifties, or the twenties, or the late 1800s. It was the kind of place where people used to store vegetables and jars and things like that. She could barely see more than a few feet in front of her—only the space illuminated by the open cellar door and then black beyond that.

They began loading the planters in, having to pile them farther and farther back. Suddenly, inexplicably, Liam closed the door and they were in darkness. There was only the tiniest crack of dim light coming from a small window on the wall to her right, covered in cardboard.

She could hear Liam breathing beside her, quiet as usual. "I just wanted to see what it feels like," he finally said. "Do you mind?" Maggie didn't tell him to open the door or say she was scared. Liam seemed comfortable with the silence, but it began to make her antsy.

"Isn't it weird how you see colors when the lights first go out?" she said, to break the silence. "Right now I can see green dots following each other. Green-dot parade."

"I just see red lines," Liam said. "Pretty standard."

"When I was a kid, it always frustrated me that when you opened your eyes, the dots disappeared," Maggie admitted. "I wanted to catch them. Weird, huh?"

"Everyone who ends up on this peninsula has some kind of issue," Liam teased. "Water Street is like the Island of Misfit Toys."

They breathed and listened to the quiet of the cellar.

"How many years old is this house?" Liam asked. "Do you know?"

"My dad said it was built in the 1880s," Maggie answered. "What are *your* issues?"

"Loving an unattainable girl my entire life," Liam said easily, without hesitation. "Who *does* that?" He didn't sound embarrassed. He seemed to want to go on, like he needed to explain himself, but it took a few seconds. "Pauline loves to go on and on about how life is short and how you have to live it up. But, I don't know, I think it's just her way of dodging real stuff sometimes." Maggie could hear his feet shifting on the dirt in the dark. "She talks about her mom being stuck in the past, on what happened with her dad, but in a way she's stuck on it too. It's like she doesn't think she has a future, just because her dad died young." Liam paused, sorting through his thoughts. "She won't make any real choices—I'll bet you anything she ends up working at the tea company all her life, because she won't decide anything big for herself. And I think her mom likes it that way. I don't think her mom wants her to grow up and find her own path or anything. She just wants her close."

"You think she'll come around to you one day?" she asked.

"To me? I doubt it. But I can't help feeling how I feel. I'm kind of a one-girl guy. I can't help it; it's like a curse, really. My dad was the same way, even though my mom didn't stick around."

There was a strange pause, and he moved closer to her. Reflexively Maggie stepped on the stair to open the cellar door and reached her arms overhead, pushing upward. Sunlight flooded in. In front of her, Liam was kneeling. He'd found something on the ground. He held it up to her. A delicate bracelet, grimy from dirt, with a tiny, cherry-shaped charm.

"I felt it with my foot," he said, and smiled, friendly. "Here, for you." In the light she could see his face was glistening with sweat from all the effort carrying the planters.

Maggie took the bracelet but didn't say anything. Turning it over in her hands, she wondered how old it was and who'd left it, how it had fallen off. But she'd never know, she guessed. Liam was watching her curiously. There were too many things to like about him. Maggie could feel her affection being bound to him like roots, and she didn't like it but didn't know how to stop it from happening. Because it came with a desire to stand closer to him, the way he smelled affecting her pulse.

Out on the grass, Liam helped her bundle up the potting-mix bags, and Maggie took hold of them in a giant armful. "Well, thanks. See you."

"Yeah." Liam turned and started walking away.

She looked at the ground just to give her eyes something

to do besides watch him walk, but just before he disappeared into the pines, she turned them on him until he'd disappeared, studying the form of his back, the outline of his arms. "Maggie, you're an idiot," she said to herself. As she walked inside, she stroked the bracelet in her palm.

Maggie's heart is a darkening red; it's slowly turning a different shade. I watch her lie awake and wait for something to plug up the hole that's opened inside her, and it makes me wish that I could tell her what I've learned, being a ghost. I've seen enough of people stretching the years to know the things we want are bigger than what we get and as deep as outer space. Looking up at the cold, empty sky beyond the cellar door, I know that our longing can stretch at least that far.

It's the bracelet that disconcerts me. It looks familiar—I already know it, where it's shiny and where it's dull. I know already that some letters are more faded than others. In other words the bracelet rings a bell, and that's a feeling I can't remember having. As Maggie holds it up to study it, I try to make out the faded name. Maybe it's my name. But I have no more luck than she does.

Through the window I can smell the air coming down from Canada, breezes full of the Arctic. If you fill your lungs deeply enough, you'll breathe the ice caps, moose breath, Eskimo campfires. A ghost town comes to mind, north of here, that was abandoned in the late 1800s—I don't know when I saw it or why. It's not the kind of ghost town you picture in the West, with tumbleweeds and shoddy, clapboard houses. It's polished and sophisticated, with an avenue of clean, white houses and a courthouse, a dry goods shop, a mayor's house, a capitol. It's so impeccably clean that it looks like all the people left just the day before. Every time I think of it, I get a lonely feeling.

I drift out of my window, to go see where they're digging the new grave of the latest victim; she'll be buried in White Stone. I float out to the old cemetery, wander among the bones I can see under the dirt— some curled in balls in their tombs, some long and stretched out like they're standing on a stage. I can hear their souls whispering in the trees sometimes. I've begun to suspect they're here after all, and closer than they've let on. My empty, invisible, nonexistent heart picks up speed. Maybe it turns a darker shade of red too—I don't know, because it isn't there.

A late, last warm-weather storm is crackling somewhere far-off—I see the faintest hints of lightning.

And suddenly I see my first ghost. He's one lonely-looking wisp of a man, sitting on a stone a few yards away; he's transparent and—just as I'd pictured—glowing. He seems to want to tell me something, but I can't hear him, and he can't hear me. "Where are all the ghosts?" I ask, but no words escape my lips. He keeps looking at me as if there's something important he wants me to know. "How can I keep people safe?" I ask. But he shakes his head. And then he floats into the woods and fades away.

I float home, over town after town, toward Gill Creek and Water Street. An occasional car drives below or a person walking through the woods or down the streets of town.

If I could show you the lives of the people below me—the colors of what they all feel heading into this chilling, late fall—they'd be green and purple and red, leaking out through the roofs, making invisible tracks down the roads.

8

THE COLD RETURNED SOMETIME THAT NIGHT AND STAYED. IT BLEW DOWN FROM the north and settled in for the winter. It blew across the fourth girl, found just before Thanksgiving in the icy slush at the edge of the lake in Sturgeon Bay. She was like the others—facedown, no sign of struggle. She had been gone a full week before turning up in the lake. Meanwhile, Gill Creek pulled together in the face of the threat. There were bake sales and benefits in honor of the families of the victims; there were indoor activities planned every Friday night for families to attend together. The town forged on with its traditions and small events: There would be a fall festival and a Turkey Gobble the weekend after Thanksgiving. "Faces of Gill Creek

Past" was on exhibit at the Maritime Museum, and that Saturday Pauline invited Maggie to go.

They rode downtown in Mrs. Boden's Mercedes, which she kept parked in the garage so that it was shiny and perfect, black as ink. Maggie marveled at the way the car smelled and how smoothly it glided down Water Street, but she also marveled that someone could spend so much money on a car. Mrs. Boden wore a brown trench coat and pressed, emerald-green pants. Her blond hair was perfectly done, and she wore red lipstick and dark eyeliner on her catlike eyes. Pauline, on the other hand, was mismatched in a long, wrinkled maroon skirt, blue boots, and a vintage green coat she'd bought at a thrift store.

Mrs. Boden asked Maggie the standard adult questions as she drove. "How's school going? You must be very self-disciplined to be homeschooled. What's your best subject?" And she acted interested in everything that Maggie answered. She kept nodding, saying "I see" or "Oh, really?" or "Good for you." But it was like they were just things to say. Pauline sat in the passenger seat looking out the window quietly.

The museum was small, but someone had put a lot of imagination into the exhibit—it consisted of several rooms through which you walked past life-size black-and-white photos of past residents of Gill Creek—dating all the way back to the time photography had been invented. Some of the photos were large, plaster cutouts—trimmed to the shape of the people they portrayed—so that their silhouettes stood in the middle of the rooms. The photos on the walls showed people in their daily lives: in front of tractors or shops, bustling down Main Street, stomping cherries at the annual Cherry Festival, the harvest queen riding in a parade.

Pauline trailed along behind her mom from photo to photo. Standing behind them, Maggie could see that Pauline emulated the way her mother tilted her head as she examined each photo, though she couldn't seem to stop her foot from tapping, clearly restless.

"Oh, Maggie, here's one of your house," Mrs. Boden said, turning and waving her toward them.

Maggie came up beside her and studied the photo, surprised and excited to see the familiar white house, though it looked different in the photo . . . of course, newer. A tiny scrawl at the lower corner indicated that the date was 1887.

A woman stood in front of it in a white Victorian dress. The photo was too grainy to make out her features perfectly, but she was beaming—her teeth big and white on her tan face. She had dark-blond hair piled to the back of her head in the Victorian way, and there was something *foreign* about her. Maggie wondered if she could be the person who'd owned the cherry bracelet. Her arms sprouted goose bumps, thinking about it. The woman looked so full of life.

A tiny label to the left of the photo said: "Katherine Gustafson, 1865–1889." She'd died young, probably not too long after the photo was taken. *How had she died? Why did she move to the middle of nowhere?* Maggie wondered.

Maggie looked up and around to find that Pauline and her mom had wandered out of sight. She walked into the next room and the next and found them in the back-most exhibit area. Pauline was looking at a photo of a fisherman and his young son standing on a commercial fishing boat. Lines were etched deep into the man's face.

Pauline's mom was raking her hands through Pauline's messy, dark hair, trying to smooth it out. Pauline kept shrugging away.

"Mom, I'm not five. You don't need to do my hair."

"I know, but you have such beautiful hair and all you have to do is brush it."

Pauline sighed and gave in, letting Mrs. Boden continue to fuss at her.

"This is my great-great-grandpa, isn't he cool?" Pauline said over her shoulder, when she saw Maggie was there, pointing to the little boy. "I like this one, because he looks so much like my dad in it." She turned to her mom. "Doesn't he remind you of Dad, Mommy? Same eyes." Maggie noticed they were Pauline's eyes too.

Her mom looked at the photo, then nodded. She looked back at Maggie and smiled, the same smile that wasn't really happy. "Maggie, don't you think Pauline's too young to have a boyfriend? This kid James keeps calling her." She was changing the subject. But Maggie didn't want to argue with someone's mom, even though Pauline was giving her the wide eyes of annoyance.

"I don't even *want* to go out with him," Pauline said.

"But are you being clear about it? Boys need things spelled out."

"If completely ignoring him is being clear about it, then yes."

Mrs. Boden looked at her, exasperated. "Can I help it if you're precious to me?"

"I'm not going out with anyone, Mom. You're like Mommie Dearest or something." Mrs. Boden gave a tinny laugh, then turned and headed back into one of the other rooms.

"It's actually a pretty good exhibit," Maggie said, making conversation.

"My mom donated twenty thousand dollars to this museum," Pauline said absently. Maggie nearly choked on her own tongue. "What, do you think that's a crazy amount?" Pauline turned to her in surprise.

"It's just, like, half my mom's salary," Maggie said.

"Oh," Pauline said, "sorry. I'm so gauche. My mom always says that."

They both turned back to the photo. "Don't they all look like hardy, noble souls? You know," Pauline said, "it's so easy to think someone's perfect when they're dead."

Maggie didn't know what to say to that. "What was your dad like, besides funny? I remember you said he was funny."

Pauline thought. "He looked out for me. It was, like, I was always safe because he was there."

Pauline fished into her pocket and a moment later pulled

out a little piece of paper. She peeled something off the back, then raised it to the image of the grown man holding the boy's hand and placed it under his nose. It was a fuzzy mustache sticker. Maggie nervously peered around behind them to see if anyone was watching.

"I'm pretty sure this guy had a sense of humor. I brought a whole pack. Let's go do the other ones," she said. "Let's do your lady too."

Afterward, walking downtown, they saw the headlines in the metal newspaper vending machines, a particularly prominent one saying "Evil Among Us."

"It's not evil," Maggie said, frustrated. "Someone's probably just bonkers. Good and evil sound so nice and simple compared to messed up, crazy brain stuff."

As they walked people looked at Pauline, especially guys. Maggie had never felt so much like the center of attention before. But Pauline seemed oblivious. She was dressed carelessly in her wrinkled, thin coat; her hair was tangled despite her mom's finger brushing. They came to a standstill in front of a bakery, peering in through the window at all the cakes.

"*I* believe in good and evil," Pauline said. She seemed distant, like she was thinking it through.

A cute guy around their age emerged from the bakery and turned to look over his shoulder at Pauline as he walked away.

"Pauline, do you notice how many people check you out?" Pauline shook her head as if shaking it off. "It doesn't mean anything. I don't care. It's stupid."

Maggie couldn't imagine what it must be like to be noticed all the time. She knew some people noticed pretty girls in a good way, and that others, like Elsa, made all sorts of negative assumptions about them—that they were conceited or bitchy or whatever other clichés went along with beauty. She guessed it was like a blessing and a curse. Still, she didn't love the way she was invisible next to Pauline. A kernel of envy lay at the pit of her stomach, and Maggie tried to dismiss it.

"Maggie, I was thinking about what you said, about your mom's salary. I know you're going to college, and you're trying to save and all that, and my family has just . . . a lot of money. My mom gives me this allowance, and I never end up spending all of it because that's not humanly possible. I have, like, eight thousand dollars in the bank."

Maggie looked over at her.

"I just . . . can I give it to you?" Pauline glanced up at her, looking embarrassed, then back at the cakes. "I'm not trying to be condescending or anything; I just really don't need it. I'll probably stick around here anyway and work for my mom. And I just . . . it's not fair. I want you to be able to use it for school, so you can be a world leader someday or something. The world needs someone like you."

Maggie felt her eyes start to prickle. She shook her head. "That's . . . that's so sweet, Pauline, but I'll be fine. Believe me, I'll be fine. I really appreciate you offering. So much."

Pauline gazed back through the window. "Okay, but if you

ever need it, just remember, the offer stands."

Maggie tried to swallow the lump in her throat and followed her gaze.

Finally Maggie looked over at Pauline and widened her eyes at her. "We should get a ton of pastries. We can take photos of ourselves eating them. Then we can do an exhibit called 'Faces of Gill Creek Eating Their Faces Off.'"

A lady walking past frowned at her; she looked like one of the museum curators.

They drove home with a bag full of napoleons and disco on the radio that Pauline had picked out and insisted on playing loudly through open windows despite the cold, with warm air blasting from the vents.

9

THE BARN WAS AFLAME AS MAGGIE AND HER PARENTS CROSSED THE PARKING lot—a block of glowing yellow squares in the dark, with twangy, lively country music escaping through the double doors. This year the town committee had turned the annual Turkey Gobble into a benefit for the families of the victims and decided to hold it at the huge, refurbished barn that sometimes doubled as a community center.

It was warm and bright inside, crowded but subdued— lots of people gathered by the dessert table and the bar, chatting and eating. As Maggie and her parents entered, the music switched to polka. Shrugging out of her coat, Maggie found Pauline and Liam hiding in a corner at the air-hockey table, completely silent. (Pauline tackled any game where she competed against him with utter seriousness.) She was wearing a headband with two wobbly turkeys attached to the ends of long, springy antennae. She didn't look up as Maggie approached; she just bit her lip as she thrust her left hand forward over and over to knock the puck back at Liam.

"Hey," Maggie said, leaning against the table. "You're going to yank your arm out of its socket." Pauline looked up, and her eyes glinted, her turkeys wobbling. Liam moved in a blur, and the puck slammed home while she was distracted.

"Game," Liam said, and straightened up with a grin. Pauline threw her paddle onto the table.

"Nice," Maggie said, pointing to Pauline's head. Pauline stared at her blankly for a minute, then seemed to remember and reached up to touch an antenna. "Thanks. They were selling them at 7-Eleven for a dollar. I got you a pair too." She reached into her giant leather bag that was slung at her back and pulled them out, then pushed them onto Maggie's head. Maggie looked around the room—everyone else was in their holiday sweaters, slacks, blazers; dressy casual. Pauline was in jeans and a sparkly tank top.

"Well, they're all here," Pauline said, gazing around. "Mayor Alex"—she pointed to a woman by the drinks table—"my third-grade teacher, the guy who owns the Coffee Moose. My mom keeps trying to get me to get up there to sing something. She thinks I'm a really good singer. You know, *moms*." Maggie's own mom and dad were over in a corner talking to a grandmotherly type in a vest. Both of her parents were great at parties, smart and interested in everyone and charming. Her mom was even tapping her foot to the polka beat. Some people were polka'ing in the back corner, and others were waiting in line at the keg. Maggie saw Gerald from the antique store on the other side of the room and quickly looked away. A group of women was gathered by the dessert table, having an animated conversation and glancing over at Liam and shaking their heads.

"Those women are talking about you," Maggie said, and pointed. Liam rubbed at his jaw, and a red tint crept up his cheeks; he seemed to be wincing a little.

"It's because of his dad," Pauline said, eyes lighting up with amusement. "He put a pumpkin carved with 666 in front of church this morning."

"He thinks he's being funny," Liam said sheepishly, looking around. "But I don't think anyone else is in on the joke."

A guy from Pauline's school came over and asked her to dance, and she went off with him. Maggie and Liam sat on the couch eating cake and watching her tilting around the room like a doe, leggy and beautiful. Everywhere the lights and shadows seemed to land on her.

"You look pretty," Liam said to Maggie, looking down at her wrist. "You wore the bracelet."

"Just trying to represent my homeys from the 1800s," she said drily. He reached down to touch it, sliding his index finger under the delicate chain. "I love it," she said more sincerely. She wasn't sure why she loved it so much—because of its mystery or where it had been found in the dark, secret heart of the house—or because Liam had found it for her. She showed him the place on the back of the cherry charm where she'd found scrawled letters: two words, clearly a first and last name, too faded to read.

Maggie sensed a shift in the air, and they both looked up. She didn't know how long Pauline had been standing there watching them. Her face was serious, and her forehead had wrinkled up—but in a moment that expression was gone, replaced by the sparkly green eyes and the smile with the spaced-apart teeth. She thrust her hand into Liam's and pulled him up to dance, and the two went off to the middle of the floor. It surprised Maggie, but they knew how to polka. They moved through the steps woodenly, as if they'd done it a hundred times before but only with each other—the same slightly off-rhythm steps, the same wrong arm movements. They weren't good at it, but they matched each other perfectly.

Maybe now was a good time to get some air.

Outside her toes froze through her boots almost immediately. Back in Chicago the cold gnawed at your bones, but here it seemed sharper. She saw a group of smokers across the lot, shivering and shuffling their feet as they talked, and recognized Hairica among them—she'd covered her effusive hair with a thick, wool hat. Maggie could hear that they were talking about the killer and who he might be. She approached and stood next to Hairica, acknowledging her with a friendly glance.

"Maybe someone escaped from the prison, down below the peninsula," someone said.

"You know that guy down on Cherry Street, Chuck Elliott? He's kind of crazy." They continued to bandy names around, all of men. One of the names that came up was Mr. Witte.

"He's a devil worshipper," a blond girl said.

"I think he was in prison for a while," some guy offered.

"My mom thinks it could be him," Hairica offered meekly.

Maggie prickled and looked at her, then around the group. "You guys shouldn't accuse people." Hairica blushed. Everyone got awkwardly silent.

"Sorry, you're right," Hairica said.

Maggie could tell she'd killed the mood, so she started backing up, turning to Hairica. "Wow, it's cold out here. I'm gonna go back."

Hairica peeled off from the group too but cut in the other direction, heading toward the edge of the lot, where, Maggie could see, a short path through the trees led to a subdivision where she must live. She waved to Maggie and left her breath trailing behind her.

Inside it took Maggie a moment to realize the shift in the mood. Everyone was silent, turned in the direction of the band, and the polka had died. Instead someone was singing, with only a guitar in the background. Maggie was shocked to realize it was Pauline.

She looked tiny up in front of the men of the band, a little embarrassed but like she belonged. Either she'd forgotten to take off her turkey headband or she'd kept it on on purpose, and it was a strange visual, because her voice was strong, full of longing, and beautiful. Maggie couldn't believe it—Pauline's voice was so husky, yet so clean, it gave her chills.

She was singing a country song Maggie had heard once on one of her mom's John Prine CDs. She didn't usually like country, but she remembered liking how bittersweet the song was, and Pauline's voice fit it perfectly.

"Make me an angel," Pauline sang, "that flies from Montgomery. Make me a poster in an old rodeo." The words didn't really make sense, but in a way they did. To Maggie it seemed like a song about wanting to be far away and also wanting to be something *more*.

Pauline went through the chorus one more time and then let her voice trail off on the last note. Abruptly she darted off the stage, her face bright red as everyone clapped.

She came straight toward Maggie, shoulders hunched. "Let's go," she said. Liam found them in the crowd and trailed along behind.

About a half hour later, they were perched on the banks of the strait, looking over at Wisconsin proper. The bridge stuck straight up against the dark sky, giving the impression that the people on the peninsula were prisoners in Alcatraz. Maggie blew on her hands, and Pauline shivered in her coat. Liam didn't seem to mind the cold at all.

"I don't understand why you're so embarrassed," Maggie said. "That was amazing."

Pauline shrugged, and Maggie thought she detected a blush rising on her cheeks. "I don't know why I let my mom talk me into it."

She wrapped her arms around herself and looked out across the strait for a while and then reached over and tagged Maggie on the shoulder. "Let's play tag. You're it."

Maggie turned. "Are you serious?"

Pauline was on her feet jumping up and down. "You're *it*!"

Maggie lunged for Pauline, who darted out of the way. She moved as if to reach for her again but sidestepped and shot her arm out to tag Liam, who was just catching on. Maggie had always dominated at tag as a kid, at any game where you had to be clever and physically fast.

She and Pauline scattered into the trees of the park as Liam came after them. He went after Pauline first, and Maggie could hear whooping and screaming in the dark. And then he reappeared, looking for her. She moved behind a big maple and stood still, trying to keep her breath low and steady.

He appeared without so much as a sound, coming around to her left. He put a hand against the side of her rib cage, trying to make out her shape in the shadows. "Tag," he said.

Maggie took a deep breath. She crossed her arms over her chest, her face prickling. "You got me." They stood awkwardly for a moment.

They walked out onto the open grass and saw that Pauline had given up the game as quickly as she'd started it and was riffling through the trunk of her car. She pulled out a huge rectangular box covered in illustrations of flowers and dragons and rockets. Fireworks.

"Let's light them over the water," she said.

"Where'd you get those?" Maggie asked.

Pauline shrugged. "Online."

"They look highly illegal. You can blow off your hands, doing this stuff," Liam said, but Pauline was carefully positioning the rockets, pointing them in the direction of the bridge and sticking their ends into the dirt.

"Have you ever seen the northern lights?" Maggie suddenly asked as Pauline finished up.

Pauline shook her head. "My dad said he did once. Right from Gill Creek. When he was little. Some weird weather pattern pushed them this way."

"I want to see them someday," Maggie said. Liam and Pauline both agreed it was a must. They all peered into the sky as if mentioning them could summon them.

Then, finally, Pauline turned to Maggie. "Do you wanna light 'em? You're the responsible one."

She handed Maggie a lighter and then took a couple of steps backward. Liam tried to argue that he should be the one to light them, but Maggie was suddenly enamored with the idea of doing it herself.

Pauline and Liam backed up. Maggie struck the matches

and timed the lightings, spacing them each a few seconds apart. Finally, with relief, she stepped back with Pauline and Liam, and they sank onto their butts on the cold ground and waited.

Whoosh. Whoosh. Whoosh.

They watched; tiny sparkles went spilling across the sky. Then nothing.

Then . . . the sky lit up, and there was a deafening series of crackles as a bright pink heart flew open far above the bridge, getting wider and wider before collapsing, its tiny pink dots plummeting earthward. It was enormous.

"Oh my God," Maggie whispered. There was no way people hadn't seen it. There was no way the entire *town* hadn't seen it.

A loud crackle muted her voice as a bright white circle of sparkly, crackly puffs flew upward, seeming to sprinkle the bridge as they fell. Gill Creek lit up against the water. Tiny in the distance, the shapes of a few scattered people gathered at the water's edge to watch.

Maggie put her hands on her ears, and that made it even better: The explosions sounded far away, muted and beautiful.

Then a purple one—it flew outward, and the shape seemed hazy for a moment but sorted itself into a giant smiley face.

Pauline laughed so loud and screechy that Liam flinched. Maggie didn't realize how big her own smile was until her cheeks started hurting. The fireworks lasted only five minutes, maybe even less, but they were spectacular. It felt like they were taking a town that was lost in the dark and lighting it up.

10

IT WAS ELSA, HAIRICA'S NEIGHBOR, WHO SAW THE COPS PULL UP TO HAIRICA'S house a couple of weeks later, on December 8, lights flashing but sirens silent. The rumors raced around by word of mouth hours before the facts appeared on the news that night.

Hairica hadn't come home the night before. And that morning her car was found empty at the side of Millers Park, her thick, wool hat nearby.

Light snow fell as Maggie crunched down Main Street that morning. To her surprise, the general store was closed, as was the Coffee Moose, where she usually got her coffee before work because it was better than the stuff Elsa brewed up. Several other sets of windows were dark that hadn't been the week before.

She was just approaching the Emporium when she saw a figure emerge, pulling the door shut and turning to lock it.

"Elsa?"

Elsa turned, startled, and then looked relieved. "Oh lord, you scared me," she breathed, holding her hand to her chest.

"Why are you locking up?" Maggie asked.

Elsa looked guilty. She wrapped her scarf more firmly around her neck and looked away, then back at Maggie. "It was a spur-of-the-moment decision. I just decided on my way in."

"What was a spur-of-the-moment decision?"

Elsa hesitated. "I'm closing up the shop for the winter."

Maggie felt her heart sink.

"Nobody comes downtown to shop these days; everyone's scared; no one's really into strolling down Main Street. Hair . . . sorry, Erica, is gone. It just . . . doesn't make any sense to stay open."

She crouched to hide the key in the spot where she always did, under a rock at the corner of the walkway.

"But . . . ," Maggie said dumbly. "I need the job—I'm saving for school. I . . ."

Elsa looked at her sympathetically and put her hand on her shoulder. "I'm sorry, Maggie, I really am." She stamped her feet and walked Maggie in the direction of her car. "You'll be the first person I call once I reopen."

Maggie stood there, at a loss for words. "Thanks," she finally managed to say.

Elsa unlocked her car, gazed around as if to make sure the coast was clear, and then looked at Maggie and sighed. "This time of year I always feel, if we can just get through the winter, we will be okay." She patted Maggie again on the shoulder and offered a smile that was meant to be encouraging. "We just have to make it till spring. Anyway, I'm sure I'll see you around town."

Maggie nodded. And then Elsa got in, spun her wheels slightly in the icy lot, and pulled away. Maggie stood in the warmth of the car exhaust and then turned back in the direction she'd come.

Even in homeschooling, there was Christmas break. Maggie woke every morning to ice crystals encrusted on the corners of her bedroom window and icicles dangling above the side porch. The grass disappeared under snow. Driving around aimlessly, she'd see people pulling Santas and sleighs and wooden nativity scenes onto their lawns. The lights on the trees in front of Gill Creek Public School and the wreaths on the courthouse kept the pulse of the peninsula steady, despite all the chaos. Next door, Mrs. Boden had hired a company to decorate her lawn with twelve glowing reindeer—as white-lit and understated as twelve reindeer could be—stretching out toward the water and turned in the direction of the lake, so passing boats could see them at night.

Sometimes Maggie thought about hiking back into the woods to check on the progress of the sauna, and instead, not wanting to run into Liam alone, trekked out in the other direction, pulling on her hat and gloves and thick, old Columbia jacket, plus her waterproof boots that were getting too small for her. (She didn't want to ask for a new pair and see her mom pretend the money didn't stress her out.)

Her parents were loathe at first to let her go into the woods alone, but Maggie was climbing the walls, and eventually they'd relented; Water Street was too isolated to be a target anyway. What was a killer going to do, Maggie had argued, drive to an isolated three-house neighborhood and wait for some victim to come trundling along through the woods where hardly anyone ever walked? She trekked into the trees on the other side of the house, out to the very tip of their tiny spit of land, and watched some Horned Grebes land on the water, mist rising from the lake against the cold air and ice creeping out from the shore inward across its surface. Pauline said if it got cold enough the lake would freeze completely, but that was still hard to believe, considering its vastness.

That weekend Pauline demanded they get out of town to the thriving metropolis of Green Bay to see the sights.

"There's a botanical garden. We should go to the railroad museum. Have you ever been to a casino?"

In the end Pauline chose an indoor theme park called Pirateville. "They have mermaids," she said matter-of-factly, reading from the website. "They're open all winter." They had a show there where women swam underwater and breathed through tubes and did acrobatics in fish tails.

"You know mermaids are imaginary, right?" Maggie said.

Pauline blinked at her innocently and then held her hands under her chin like Ariel. "They're doing *The Little Mermaid*."

Pirateville—which on the map had looked huge, with a Pirate's Cove and a Marauder's Cavern—was tiny and poky. The log-flume ride, which had been drawn as a raging river, was closed, a miniature wave lagoon lapped against its cement walls forlornly, and the mermaid theater smelled weird. They entered at ground level and climbed down into old, upholstered movie seats, facing a curtain that, Maggie assumed, concealed the glass walls of the large water tank.

The curtains opened. The water was lit Day-Glo blue from above, and the Little Mermaid was there, swimming around and breathing through her tube, dancing in the water and lip-synching to the sound track. Maggie looked over at Pauline, who was captivated.

The production ended up being really good. They did the original Hans Christian Andersen version of the story—the tragic, non-Disney-fied one, where the prince marries another woman and treats the Little Mermaid like an adopted daughter, causing her to stab herself with a dagger made of her own hair.

"Well, glad we saw something cheerful," Maggie said, on the drive back.

Pauline looked crushed. "My dad used to read the real story to me. But I guess he left out the bad bits." Pauline dabbed at the corner of her eye with a pinkie.

"You are *not* crying."

"No." Pauline shook her head. But sure enough her eyes were wet with tears. She snorted with embarrassed laughter, and then Maggie burst into laughter too.

After a while of driving in silence, Pauline spoke. "You know, I thought about inviting Liam, but things have been weird with us lately."

Maggie thought and then steeled her courage. "Pauline, why haven't you ever . . . you know? Liked Liam, like that?"

Pauline looked over at her thoughtfully. She lolled her head to the side, then fiddled with the visor. "I'm not into anyone that way. I don't know. I just, I don't see why everyone has to pair off and fall in love and everything anyway. Why can't we just stay the way we are?"

Maggie picked at her fingernails while Pauline went on.

"My mom, she'll never get over that my dad died. She'll hold on to it forever. It's like, her treasure, like she's a dragon and missing my dad is all these giant rubies she's guarding or something. I mean I love her. It's just, she's consumed by it." Pauline inscribed smooth semicircles around the steering wheel with her hands, from the top to the bottom then the bottom to the top. "That's what it's like to love someone."

Maggie studied her. She usually seemed so completely carefree, but at this moment she looked sad and lost and older. Pauline seemed to come back to herself, suddenly self-conscious. She waved a hand like she was shooing a fly. "I just don't feel that way about him anyway."

Maggie nodded. Pauline didn't have any reason to lie. So she didn't know why thinking of Liam felt secret. Like something she should keep hidden, like Mrs. Boden's dragon rubies.

"Do you know today's the shortest day of the year?" Pauline said, changing the subject.

Maggie shook her head. "I didn't."

"It's the twenty-first. I always keep track of it. Because now the days start getting longer. That always makes me feel better."

Maggie impulsively patted the top of Pauline's head affectionately, thinking how she only kept track of the good things.

A little after 6:00 a.m. on Wednesday, a girl showed up at the Gill Creek police station, bruised and shivering. Erica "Hairica" Lasstrom had hiked all the way from the forest that bordered Zippy's Amusement Park, where she'd been held in a small trailer on the grounds, because she was too terrified to flag down a car.

It was her long hair that had allowed her to escape. Her attacker had grabbed it, and she'd yanked herself away, leaving a tuft of it in his hands as he tumbled off balance. She'd hidden in the woods all night, too scared to move. In the morning she'd gotten turned around among the trees and lost, finally coming to a road and hiking the four miles to the police station, scratched and bruised but alive.

In the paper, she described her attacker as male, tall, and muscular. He'd kept her eyes covered and put her in some kind of van. He didn't say a thing to her the whole time except for "Get in," but she swore he had an accent. Details of her captivity were not disclosed.

The police questioned several suspects and searched the amusement park, which had been abandoned years before. No arrests were made.

11

MAGGIE AND HER PARENTS ALWAYS HAD A DATE TO DECORATE THE TREE together. Her mom had worked a miracle this year, finding a tree practically for free at Lowe's, minus a few branches and more than a little dry. Already it had left a wreath of needles around itself on the floor of the living room. Her mom had made homemade eggnog and had put Nat King Cole on the stereo, because it was important to her—she always said— that Maggie could rely on traditions. She'd also bought a mountain of tinsel, more tinsel than any one family should decently own, and lit a roaring fire in the study fireplace.

They were just beginning the first stage of tree decorating—they always put the glass balls on after the lights—when there was a knock at the door. Pauline stood on the landing outside the kitchen. Maggie opened the door.

"Hi, Pauline," her mom called from the living room. "Come decorate with us."

Pauline stayed on the landing. "Hey, Mrs. Larsen, sorry I can't, I have to get back. I just wanted to ask Maggie something really quick."

She stepped just inside the door and looked at Maggie secretively, lowering her voice.

"Liam wants to take me to this place for my Christmas present on Tuesday. It's like this ice hotel where you can have dinner at this ice restaurant. Anyway, I really want to go, but we couldn't get back by curfew. I wonder if I could just tell my mom I'm hanging out at your house? And if she calls or something, you could just say I fell asleep? We'll be home by ten, eleven latest," she said.

Maggie shifted from foot to foot. She wasn't a good liar. And she didn't like the idea of Pauline and Liam being out after curfew anyway, with everything going on. But she nodded.

"Okay."

Pauline swallowed.

"I think he's planning to give me *the talk*," she said.

Maggie felt taken aback. "What talk?" she asked, though she had a twisting feeling that she knew.

Pauline wrapped her arms around herself.

"You know, tell me he loves me, make me choose whether to be with him or not. He keeps hinting that it's now or never."

Pauline looked tired and a little drawn.

Maggie didn't know what to say.

"I don't want to lose him as a friend, you know?" Pauline said. "I don't want to hurt him." She stamped her feet, frustrated, knocking off snow. "Anyway, thanks, Maggie. I owe you."

"No problem."

Pauline darted forward and kissed her on the cheek. "You're the best." She turned and ran back to her house.

Back inside Maggie drank her eggnog and helped with the tinsel. Her parents were both in an excellent mood, and her mom even put a dash of rum in her drink. "Next year you can have two dashes," she said wryly, and Maggie laughed and said, "Be still my heart." But she felt unsettled. Her dad disappeared for a moment and came back with a package in green wrapping, laying it in Maggie's lap.

"Early present," he said.

Maggie could feel that it was clothes. For a moment she thought with a thrill that she knew what it was. She pulled at the wrapping, revealing tissue paper, red with white stripes like the awning of the store downtown, and her pulse picked up. Within that, a familiar fabric. But it was the sight of that that sank her hopes. It was a blue silk pattern with fuchsia flowers. It was the ugly dress from the store.

"I know you wanted the other one more," her dad said uncertainly, almost shyly. "I was hoping this one would be a good second best."

Maggie held the dress up to her. She could feel her eyes start to water in sudden hurt—both because her dad was so clueless and because he was so thoughtful. She fought back the tears.

"I love it," she said brightly. And she really did, because of what it meant. But that didn't stop it from breaking her heart.

Two nights later Maggie watched Liam and Pauline pull out of the driveway.

Maggie never found out what happened between Pauline and Liam that night. All she knew, later, was how it all ended.

She knew that they hadn't gotten home by ten or eleven. And that Mrs. Boden didn't call but came over and knocked on the Larsens' door to bring her daughter home. And of course, Pauline was not there. Mrs. Boden hadn't said anything to Maggie, just tightened her lips and walked back to her house. And Maggie, watching the clock, began to worry. Telling herself they were just being flaky and would be home soon, she fell asleep, but it was a light, uneasy sleep.

She was awakened by red and blue lights at about 12:30 a.m. She watched from her window as one after another police car pulled up, too scared to move much, just rubbing her fingers nervously against the edges of the windowpane as she peered out. *Please, God, let them be okay*, she kept saying. *I'll do anything, just please let them come back.* Her heart beat fast, and her skin prickled in fear, turning hot and cold.

Hour after hour crept by. Two more cop cars arrived, and she could hear her parents making coffee downstairs and lighting a fire in the fireplace to warm the drafty rooms, but she pretended she was still asleep, and they never came to wake her. She watched the police spread out to search the area around Water Street, the woods, and along the banks of the lake, their flashlights pricking through the darkness of the trees. Had they found the car down the road with no one in it? Were they just being extra cautious? She watched her mother cross the lawn, bringing a thermos of coffee to Mrs. Boden, who sat on the porch. She couldn't bring herself to go out; she was paralyzed, frozen to her spot, watching the road for any sign of Pauline coming home, praying she'd see her figure coming up the drive any minute.

Around 2:00 a.m. a car came creeping down Water Street with its lights out, pulling up silently. Maggie could make out the vague shape but not the kind of car. It stopped at the end of the driveway, and the driver turned off the engine. But for several minutes, no one got out. Whoever it was, they'd seen the cops, who were slowly making their way toward the car.

Finally both doors opened at once, and two figures emerged. They converged at the front of the car and walked forward uncertainly.

Maggie sank in relief, felt the heat of her muscles relaxing, and said a silent prayer of thanks.

Mrs. Boden stood on the edge of the porch looking like

she might crack. Liam and Pauline looked dazed in the headlights of one of the police cars.

Liam reached for Pauline's hand. Maggie couldn't see whether Pauline reached back for his or not, because one of the cops approached them and obscured the view.

The next morning Pauline's mother drove her to the morning bus to Milwaukee.

Maggie didn't get to say good-bye.

Time has pulled me forward. It's late winter, maybe early spring. The earliest trees are just about to bud— it's that time of year, when warmth seems miles away, and yet it's starting to arrive.

I see something I don't want to see.

A girl is lying dead on the ice, with her long, dark hair across her face and a bracelet with a cherry charm on her wrist. A boy is lying in a silo on the shore. The air is freezing; it must be ten degrees below zero. I can't bear it. And as quickly as I arrive, I'm gone.

I see an owl flying above. Its wings are so wide and dark, they seem to be scraping the clouds off the sky. There's a tickle on my elbow, but I ignore it. I'm a regular halfway house for moths these days. They try to make me laugh, crawling wherever I'm ticklish, all over my invisible parts. They cover my nonexistent elbows and knees. They perch on my empty face. If you looked at me from far away, you might see I'm slowly becoming a person-shaped gathering of moths.

I glimpsed two more ghosts today. They were out on the lake, floating across the water and lit up like beacons. As they got closer, I saw it was a lady in a long, black dress and a man in what looked like a blue captain's uniform. I tried to wave to them, but they were headed somewhere, and I couldn't catch up, *and maybe they didn't see me anyway. They flashed on down along the shore and were gone.*

Now I float over the chimney of the Larsen house, sinking down. I watch the smoke trickle out, and I can see the colors of the burning wooden souls of trees: They float up in a riot of red, blue, yellow . . . trees grown up in the sun and some from low-lying marshes, some that were once pecked by woodpeckers, I can see it all.

Sinking down into the cellar, I see that the pinprick of light has gotten bigger, and it doesn't surprise me. It grows every day. Each inch brings me closer to fear. It crosses my mind, sometimes, that maybe I'm Pesta, the goddess of death. Maybe I've come to collect. I could be the scariest thing here.

I keep thinking, What's a few months in a teenaged life, compared to other things that I've seen come marching into the peninsula? *Dinosaurs, glaciers, people living in sea caves, millions of years of organisms. And Pauline and Maggie and Liam are just tiny specks in it all. Why do they seem so large?*

12

Pauline,

You said you wanted real paper letters, so here you go.
Here, things are the same. There were two features in the
paper yesterday: a Canada goose was rescued at Millers
Park (I know you'll be relieved), and they are now setting
up a checkpoint at the bottom of Door County to stop any
suspicious-looking vehicles, whatever those are. Just don't
try to drive home in a big pedo van with tinted windows,
okay? Speaking of which, will you ever come home?

There are icicles lining the roof of my entire house. It
looks like a fortress and even my dad is scared of getting

impaled by one. They say it's gonna be the coldest winter we've had since 1823, thanks to climate change.

Not the same here without you.

Love, Liam

Pauline,

How's life in the tea trade? We're putting in new banisters that won't wobble in a deadly, toss-you-down-the-stairs kind of way. It's freeze-your-butt-cheeks cold here, but I guess it's the same in Milwaukee. But I'm also getting out of the house like you always talk me into doing. My parents and I are going to the Ice Festival in Sturgeon Bay, actually. My dad is the person small-town festivals were made for.

The big news is I got early admission into North-western. I'm going to make a buttload of money when I graduate and travel the world, and since you're already rich, you'll be able to afford to come with me. We'll live it up someday soon.

I'm including a bracelet in this envelope. It came from our cellar, and I want you to have it. I really love it, and I miss you, and it just seems like it belongs to you. I can't explain it.

Write back—Mags

Pauline,

Did you get my last letter? Here's a dry flower I found in the yard—it's crazy that it lived so long! Well, until I came along and picked it ha ha ha. I'm doing some new carving on the roof of the sauna, because it's not quite perfect yet. I think a lot about the night before you left. I hate writing, but remember I'm thinking about you. So write back.

Liam

Pauline,

Is it as cold in Milwaukee as it is in Gill Creek? I think at least two of my organs froze last night walking from the car to the house, I'm guessing liver and spleen. Are you ever coming back? Sometimes don't you feel like so much of the time you're just waiting and then waiting some more? I'm actually starting Anna Karenina *because Liam's dad shamed me into it. I know, glutton for punishment.*

Liam wants to know if you are reading his letters? Are you ignoring him?

Maggie

Maggie,

My aunt and I flew to Florida for a long weekend, so sorry I didn't write back till now. It's strange, on the plane, people just sitting there listening to their iPhones and drinking ginger ales. Everybody acts like it's not some kind of crazy miracle to be looking down at the clouds. People are so oblivious. Anyway, my mom says I can come home when things are safer back home. Who knows when that will ever happen. I miss you so much. You're the only person I can talk crazy with. Don't read too much—it will ruin your eyes.

Pauline

13

PAULINE LOST THE TIP OF HER FINGER AT HER AUNT'S TEA FACTORY. THAT WAS the first casualty of her life in Milwaukee. The second casualty was what some would have called more of a gain than a loss: She got herself a boyfriend.

Pauline's aunt lived in a penthouse apartment in a highrise, looking down on the highway that swooped south to Chicago.

For Pauline—she said in her long letters, which arrived in envelopes she made herself out of magazine pages—the weeks themselves took on a grayness. She missed the fields and the cardinals hopping around in the snow, open views, and the beauty of the lake. She was adjusting okay to her new school. Her aunt was grooming her to move in and learn to take over the tea factory someday, and the prospect depressed her.

The factory made all kinds: Earl Grey, Assam, Prince of Wales. The tea dust got in Pauline's nose and in the wet corners of her eyes, so that every Saturday and Sunday night when she came home, washing her face made the white washcloth gray. She was learning from the bottom up: Her first job was to stand on the assembly line and hold down the tops of the tea bags so that they went evenly into the machine that sewed the holes together. She was standing there daydreaming when she let her hand wander in too close, and that was how she came to lose the fingertip.

It's not that bad, she wrote. *I think it's kind of unique.*

Apparently, when he heard through the school grapevine that Pauline had been in the hospital in Milwaukee to get her finger sewn up, James Falk sent her a dozen stargazer lilies, a flower she said she'd never seen before that day but which was the most beautiful she'd ever laid eyes on.

Pauline was still utterly uninterested in James. A fact that he took in stride the first time he visited (on the pretext of being in the city to see his cousin), even when Pauline told him point blank she wasn't attracted to him. The second time, she told him bluntly that he was too boring, and apparently—she wrote—he liked her all the more for it. Her indifference only seemed to charm him, and he showed up again and again—making the long drive from Gill Creek on lots of Red Bull. Pauline said she had never been so doggedly chased by someone before. Aunt Cylla adored him.

From the sound of it, Aunt Cylla made Pauline's mom look like a wild optimist.

Here's some of her favorite advice, Pauline wrote.

"You're no different from anyone else."

"Too soon old, too late smart."

But she was also loving, and gave Pauline the best bedroom, with a window that looked out across the city. Pauline wrote in so much detail—as if hungry to get it all down—that Maggie could picture it all vividly. They played cards at night, and Aunt Cylla asked Pauline all sorts of questions about James and told her to watch out for men. The only man Cylla had ever loved was a fluffy dog named Oscar that was permanently attached to her lap.

Pauline wrote, in her typical melodramatic way, that the grayness of the neighborhood seemed to stretch around the whole world, even though it belonged just to her. It seemed to her like gray was the color of being realistic. Finally, she let James Falk kiss her and then wrote Maggie a long letter— mentioning the kiss only briefly.

I know it sounds crazy, but I think I'm different from everyone else. Most people want to move forward, but not me. I just want to come home. I just wish I was little again.

Anyway, Mom and Aunt Cylla are both adamant. I can't come home until the killer is caught. And the way things are looking, that will be never.

It sucks, because there are no Maggies here, at least

not any good ones. You've got a stout heart, Maggie. Mine feels like a raisin sometimes. That's right, I said "stout heart." I got that from The Lord of the Rings. *I've watched it three times so far because it's the only DVD Aunt Cylla owns. When Aragorn says that about the Hobbit, it reminds me of you.*

Maggie didn't know how she liked being compared to a hobbit.

All the Maggies here have hearts like these, Pauline went on.

She drew a droopy, anemic-looking heart.

She didn't ask anything about Liam.

Since Hairica, Maggie's mom rarely let her go into town anymore, even in the daytime. "Just until this whole thing's over. I wish we could send you away to a rich aunt to keep you safe, but since we can't, you're stuck with us at home."

With no job and no schoolwork for break and no Pauline, Maggie had very little to do, except deal with Abe. Pauline had had to leave him behind, and he'd adopted Maggie, waiting outside the front door every morning for her to wake up and come downstairs—his tongue lolling to one side, his breath steaming into the air. She fed him and took him on her runs with her, and he gave himself the job of being her protector, chewer of her shoes, and invader of her room, when he managed to get into the house. She didn't call Liam. She figured he was probably as bored as she was, but it didn't feel right to see him without Pauline.

And then one afternoon, he showed up on her porch.

"There's a place just behind my house where it's frozen solid," Liam said. "Let me take you."

They walked into the pine woods, Liam in front and Abe in the rear. Most guys Maggie knew would have turned back to help her over logs or held back branches to let her pass, but Liam just trudged along, and Maggie had to hold up her hands to ward off the pine branches that snapped toward her and threw snow in her eyes.

He stopped a few feet in front of her, and she caught up beside him to see they were standing at the lake's edge, the ice creeping across the water in long, bluish-white fingers.

"I've already tested it; it's fine. We're only going a few feet out. Abe . . ." Liam turned to the dog, who was sitting at the edge of the ice with ears down nervously. Liam pointed in the direction of Pauline's house. "Go home. Go on." Abe looked up at Maggie mournfully, hesitated a moment, and then slunk off into the trees again.

Liam stepped out onto the ice, and Maggie followed.

As a person who was afraid of drowning, walking on water in its frozen form was still far from comforting. But Liam's confidence helped to reassure her, and they walked only ten or so feet out before they came to a hole he'd chiseled in the ice. He'd built a windbreak on one side and left bags of snacks and a flannel blanket curled up in a ball.

"You've been fishing already?" she asked.

"Every night this week," Liam said. Maggie tried to suppress a laugh. There were no guys she knew like Liam in the world.

He showed her how to bait her hook, and she fished uselessly for about twenty minutes. Every time she got a nibble, she either pulled too fast or waited too long. Liam was endlessly patient.

"Has Pauline written you?" he asked.

Maggie nodded. "You?"

Liam shook his head. Maggie realized this meant he didn't know about Pauline and James. She thought about telling him. But then, it wasn't her news to tell.

"You know, this one time she made me help her set all these chickens free from a chicken factory in Sturgeon Bay, when we were twelve. They were all in this giant coop. We snuck over on our bikes in the middle of the night. We opened all the doors, and they all went flying everywhere, and we came home covered in feathers. And the feathers got into everything. I bet there are still feathers in my house." Liam sighed, remembering it. "She gouged her back pretty bad, crawling under a fence. She's still got a big scar."

Maggie remembered the scar, and now she pictured a twelve-year-old Pauline shimmying under a fence like a criminal. She tried to picture the chickens flying off into the dark, hundreds of them, their bright white feathers flapping and swirling in the moonlight, the sound of their wings drilling into the silent air.

"Can you imagine the people who lived nearby, looking outside in the middle of the night because of all the noise and seeing a stampede of chickens running across their yards?" Liam asked.

Maggie laughed.

"But you know," Liam went on thoughtfully, "probably most of the chickens died or got caught. It was dumb; she didn't think it through. Pauline breaks things just as much as she fixes them. But it doesn't stop her."

They sat for over an hour, until Maggie's butt had gone completely numb.

"Well, it's getting late. And I wanna show you something else."

They stood up and began walking. Maggie's feet suddenly slid, one backward, one forward. And then a *whoosh*, and her back foot plunged into the ice as it crackled around her.

Liam grabbed her just as her other foot went under. One moment she had nothing beneath her toes, and the next they were stumbling forward and on solid ground again, but not before Maggie's feet had gotten dunked in the slushy, frozen water.

"I'm so sorry," Liam said. "Here."

He crouched for her to climb on his back. Maggie balked.

"Come on, you don't want to walk through snow with wet feet."

"I'm heavier than I look."

"Yeah, right."

Once she had her arms around his neck and her thighs around his waist, Liam rose easily, like she weighed nothing.

He walked back in the direction of his house, but instead of turning home, he veered right. Maggie could feel the warmth of his back against her stomach and smell his Liamness, the smoky, musky smell that seemed part outdoors and part just *guy*.

Maggie was just about to ask where they were going when the woods became familiar and she recognized the glade up ahead and, in the middle of it, steam rising from the finished sauna.

"This is where I was taking you anyway."

He let her slide off, stood back, beamed proudly yet also shyly, and opened the door. A cloud of steamy heat enveloped her.

Maggie looked at him questioningly and then hobbled inside on her cold feet. He followed her in, closing the door behind him.

There was a bench on either side of the tiny room, and the whole place smelled deliciously of cedar. Maggie sank onto the bench to her right and shrugged out of her coat, pulling off her hat as Liam did the same. She felt the warm, wet air—thick and smelling like sweet, burned wood—sink into her skin, and her muscles relaxed. Her dark hair got damp quickly, and she wiped it aside from where it was pasting itself to the sides of her face. She rested her head back and stared up at the ceiling, listening to the dripping sounds of the moisture.

"Liam, it's like summer in here. You found a way to bring summer to winter."

She glanced over at him. He smiled, looking gratified. "You like it?"

"It's . . . the best." Her whole body felt limp and happy. She pulled off her scarf and her thermal shirt while Liam stoked the fire at the back, which was in a metal, racklike box low to the ground.

"I feel like nothing bad could find us here," she said.

Liam sat again and lifted her feet across his lap, toward the fire. "We should warm up your feet."

"Aren't you supposed to stay away from really hot stuff when your feet are frozen?" she asked.

"I think that's just if you have frostbite." He began to rub her feet. "I read that you're supposed to just put the person's feet against your belly to warm them up."

"Is there anything you don't know?" she teased.

He rolled his eyes as if to say she was one to talk, lifted his shirt, and pulled it over her feet so that her soles were touching his stomach. "There."

Steam began to fill the sauna, and Maggie, a little shy about her feet against Liam, tried to relax again. They were silent for several seconds. She tried to think of whether Pauline would mind if she saw them right now.

"Technically you're supposed to get naked in saunas,"

Liam said, with a wry grin, and Maggie smacked him on the arm.

"*Mmm-hmm*. Very subtle."

"Just kidding." Liam blushed all the same.

Impulsively, without saying anything, Maggie shimmied out of her shirt, down to just her sports bra. Liam looked at the wall; then they both laughed.

"I'm not embarrassed," Maggie said, even though it wasn't like her. "Sports bras aren't like real bras." She wasn't trying to flirt. She just wanted to be . . . different from how she usually was.

"Why would you ever be embarrassed? You look perfect."

"I don't want to be perfect," she blurted out. "I mean, ugh, I always try to be perfect."

"It's a compliment." Liam checked her feet under his shirt. "They're still a little cold." He pulled out her left foot and rubbed it, paying close attention to what he was doing. He seemed to be weighing something in his mind.

It reminded Maggie of the first day they'd met, when they'd been so comfortable sitting together and not saying anything. But the difference was Liam's hands on her feet, and a kind of intimacy in the way he was touching them— like he was concentrating, trying to think what would feel best, his thumbs kneading the backs of her heels, then, more softly, the fragile, sensitive flesh of her arches.

"They're warm now. I guess I'll walk you home," he finally said abruptly.

"Yeah," Maggie said, pulling her shirt and her coat on in two quick movements. They were so warm that the air didn't even feel cold when they walked outside.

At her door Liam told her he'd see her tomorrow. "With Pauline going the way she did, we didn't really celebrate New Year's," he said. "We should have a belated one. I'll think of something." As if they'd decided they'd see each other every day. As if, without Pauline, they would be an automatic pair.

At his house the next night, they got snacks from the fridge and a bag of cheese popcorn, and Liam led Maggie down the hall toward his room.

"Dad's asleep. He goes to bed at eight and wakes up at five. *Old guys.*" Maggie thought that Liam looked pretty wiped out himself, and she wondered why. There were circles under his eyes, and his expression was soft and sleepy.

His room was at the end of the hall. It was neat and small and smelled like Liam, with an old model ship hanging in the window and, strung across an antique wooden desk against one wall, a bunch of tools—wire cutters, a level—things Maggie recognized from helping her dad work on their house. The gramophone was on the right side of his bed.

Liam turned to her. "Okay, you have to sit here." He put his hands gently on her shoulders and guided her to his bed, then waited for her to sit and settle against the pillows he'd already propped up.

"Okay," he said again, nodding, biting his lip. He walked

around the bed and crouched toward what looked like a speaker that sat on the floor near the gramophone, propped up diagonally against the wall. The speaker was covered with a material of some kind that he'd taped on at the sides, and a mirror was glued or taped on top of the material, right in the middle. Liam checked the tape, touched the corners of the mirror, and then stood and pulled something tiny off his desk. Finally he turned to the gramophone.

"So this has been the big part, modifying the gramophone to connect to the speaker," he said, glancing at her. "Lots of soldering." He raised his eyebrows at her as if this were mock-impressive. "I stayed up pretty late." He wound the gramophone and then set the needle down. A jazzy, old record began to play through the speaker. It was Frank Sinatra's "New York, New York."

Liam sank onto the bed beside her, against the other pillows. She looked at him quizzically. "It's a random song, I know. I just thought it was festive."

He turned out the light beside his bed, held out the small, silver thing in his hand—which Maggie now saw was a laser pointer—and turned it on, pointing it at the mirror on the speaker. Then he leaned over and turned up the speaker.

Suddenly red lights appeared on the ceiling, bouncing off the mirror, as it was tilted upward, and splitting apart. Maggie stared up at them, confused, amazed. And then the lights began to dance.

They danced in rhythm with the beats from the speaker, leaping up at the low notes, getting lower at the high notes, jerking and swaying, depending on the speed of the notes.

Beside her, Liam was careful not to rub arms with her, but he kept looking over at her to see what she thought.

Maggie felt a lump of gratitude forming in her throat. It was hard to swallow. Life felt suddenly so beautiful.

"You remembered what I said about capturing the dots," she said.

Liam smiled. "I just thought, this is your first New Year's away from Chicago, and possibly your first belated New Year's ever. I don't want you to feel that it doesn't measure up. Especially since Pauline isn't here. I thought maybe you'd be happy if I caught some dots for you."

"It measures up," Maggie said, watching the lights dance across the ceiling like little red stars, like Mexican jumping beans. "It's the best, Liam. Thank you."

They sat in silence until the song was over. Maggie clapped. Liam looked sheepish but happy. "There's only one song on each side of the record," he explained.

"That was perfect," Maggie said.

"I guess it's kinda weird. I mean, I guess it lives up to how people think me and my dad are so weird, when we do stuff like this."

"Every village has got a few idiots," Maggie offered. "Don't worry about them."

Liam looked slightly convinced. They scooted down farther, so that they were lying down, staring at the now-still dots on the ceiling.

She could hear him breathing.

He looked at her in the dark. "She still hasn't written," Liam said. "I miss her."

Maggie wasn't surprised he'd said it. And she meant it when she replied, "I miss her too."

Soon his breath slowed, and he drifted off to sleep. Maggie wanted with all her being to stay, but instead she slipped out of the covers, her heart thudding as she moved away from his warm body, and hiked home under the stars.

14

THURSDAY EVENING, BECAUSE MAGGIE WAS GOING STIR-CRAZY, HER DAD SAID she could go into town to the library to pick up some books they had on hold.

"We can't keep her home all the time," he said to her mom, who looked up from some papers she'd brought home from work. "We're practically *pushing* her into the arms of the mysterious Liam Witte, who we've never even met."

Maggie felt her face flame red. Her dad seemed delighted at this reaction.

"The past couple years, I was thinking you might be gay," her dad said. "To be honest, I was kind of hoping you were gay. I was a teenage boy once. I know what they're thinking."

"Oh my God, Dad, stop talking." Her mom stifled a laugh.

She handed Maggie her keys and shooed her out the door. Maybe that had been her dad's plan all along.

Maggie drove slightly below the speed limit, because she'd learned that you never knew when you might hit an ice slick. She was becoming an expert at navigating the wintry, country roads. Downtown was the proverbial ghost town: Only the library and the convenience store were open. Maggie parked in the lot at the far end of Main Street and started walking, pulling her coat tighter against her and cursing herself for not bringing her hat. The hood of her coat just wasn't cutting it; cold air slipped in through the sides and gnawed at her ears.

At the end of Main, the library was lit up like a beacon, still festooned with evergreen garlands and red ribbons and silver bells. It was corny, but Maggie was getting used to the quaintness of downtown; she kind of liked it.

Inside she picked up her mom's books from Lillian the librarian, who—by now—knew her by name, and then turned and hurried back down Main Street. She decided to veer off to the left to the convenience store to get a Snickers, and then she cut down the side street that led diagonally back to Main.

The sound of footsteps off to the left behind her made her halt for a moment and look over her shoulder, but she figured it must just be the echo of her feet, because there was no one there, just garbage cans, dark windows, empty shops. The trees along the front of some of the storefronts swayed in the frigid breeze. She started up again, a little faster, a bit spooked but knowing she was just being twitchy.

She turned right, and behind her the footsteps continued. They sounded too slightly off to be just the echoes of her own footfalls, but whenever she looked back, the street was empty. *This is what mass hysteria feels like*, she told herself. She thought of Elsa. Elsa thought she was being followed or stalked practically four days out of seven.

Maggie took the next left, cutting away from Main, not sure why, except that she had some vague idea she didn't want to end up at the parking lot alone if someone really was following her. She threw another glance back over her shoulder—nothing but the glare of a streetlight and an empty block. Still, she felt like someone was there, just beyond the trees.

She walked faster. Up ahead the Emporium came into view, and Maggie suddenly remembered the hidden key. She walked as if she'd planned to pass the building, but at the last moment cut left, down the sidewalk that was sheltered on one side by big holly bushes.

Darting around to the side door and looking behind her, she crouched near the landscaping rocks which were dusted in snow, turning them over one by one. Which one had it been? *Which one?*

She pulled off her mittens to get a better grip, her hands prickling and trembling.

Her breath hissed in relief as she revealed, under the fifth rock she tried, the key, clumped with dirt. Glancing down the sidewalk and through the cracks of holly bushes (which revealed nothing), she scrambled up to the door and quietly turned the key in the lock, letting out her breath when it turned easily. Within a moment she was inside and locking the door behind her.

She crouched in the dark and then ducked over behind a display table, where she could look out the window from beside a large, old, brass clock that still, she knew from the vendor, kept perfect time. "You're being ridiculous," she whispered to herself. She watched through the window as the snow fell lightly. Nothing. She looked around behind her. The shadows of all the old things stuck up in crooked angles. Elsa had covered some of the stalls in drop cloths, so that only dim outlines of the shapes underneath showed through.

Outside, Main Street remained empty. She was beginning to feel like a complete moron. If only someone normal would walk by, then she could slip out with them. She could get back in her car and write off the whole thing as the insulated-town-induced paranoia it probably was. Even she, Maggie Larsen the realist, was not immune.

And then she heard it, the light tapping of glass. Inside the Emporium.

Maggie felt physically unable to move. She turned her neck, ever so slightly, toward the noise. A shadow was sliding back and forth, up and down the third, winding aisle. It reached forward, flicking a switch, and suddenly the corner was flooded with light, falling on the form of Elsa with a coffeepot in her hand.

"Elsa!" Maggie breathed in relief. Elsa jumped and simultaneously threw her hand over her heart. The coffeepot dropped and landed against a drop cloth with a *thwap*, miraculously staying intact.

"Oh my God, you scared me!" she said.

"You scared *me*." Maggie straightened up.

"What are you doing in here, honey?" Elsa turned on another lamp, then another. There was no shortage of available light in an antiques store.

Maggie looked outside. Had she imagined the footsteps? The presence following her? "I got spooked. And I knew where the key was."

"Oh, honey, I understand *that*." Elsa lifted up a retro mannequin and moved it to her left. "I had to come get this to ship because it sold on eBay. What do you think? Why do you think anyone would want this horrible, old thing?"

Maggie shrugged and smiled, relief flooding her. Elsa turned on more lights, flicking switches by the register, and each light that came on seemed to dispel the fear until it was gone. Maggie was finding tempests in teacups, as her dad liked to say about her mom whenever she stressed out too much over things that were mostly in her mind.

"Let's have some coffee," Elsa said. It was her answer to everything. Soon the pot was percolating and bubbling and filling the room with the comforting smell, and when Elsa handed Maggie a cup, she took it gladly, even though she didn't normally like Elsa's coffee.

"So what have you been up to?"

"Not much. Schoolwork."

"That's it?"

"What do you mean that's it?"

"Well, you're sixteen! Surely there's some drama."

"Elsa, all the sixteen-year-olds are trapped indoors. There's zero drama. I mean, there's . . ."

She thought about Liam and the sauna and the night in his bed with the laser show, and it must have been written on her face, because Elsa grinned.

"Who is he?" she asked.

"Nobody. Nothing is happening. Zero." Maggie looked over at one of the antique clocks, and even though it didn't tell the right time, she pretended to gauge it. "Well, I'd better get home. My parents will be wondering." Just as she turned to go, Elsa spoke.

"Maggie, I'll tell you this: Things don't just land in your lap. You have to throw yourself out there. If you just hang back protecting yourself, one day you'll find yourself my age, with a really nice garden and a really nice shop and not much else to show for it."

"I like this shop. You seem to have a pretty good life."

Elsa gave her a knowing look, waiting for the truth.

"It's nothing," Maggie said. "Really."

For a moment Elsa had started to seem like some kind of cipher of wisdom. But now she pulled out an old *Us Weekly* and began to flip through it as if she had nowhere else better to be.

"It better not be your friend Liam Witte," she said absently. "My friend Mary said she saw Mr. Witte burying a small animal over by the church. And you know killing small animals is always a stepping-stone to . . ." Elsa made a slit with her hand across her neck.

Maggie sighed. No ciphers of wisdom here.

That night she slipped outside while her parents were watching TV and went for a walk. She stood outside Liam's house with her heart pumping, Abe at her side, willing herself to knock on his window.

Her cell vibrated. For the first time seemingly ever, she had a signal. She bit down hard on her lip in surprise. It was Liam.

"Hey," he said, when she answered. His voice sounded soft, like he was lying on his couch.

"Hey," Maggie said.

They were both silent for a few seconds. "What are you doing?" Liam asked.

"Watching TV." Maggie stared around at the dark forest. "What are you doing?"

"Same."

More silence. Maggie thought about what Elsa had said, about ending up with comfort and safety but nothing else to show for it.

"Well, actually, sorry, I gotta go, my mom wants me," she

said. The quiet of the woods enveloped her. "See you later?"

"Okay. See you later."

"Okay."

The next night her mom and dad sat in the living room watching *Antiques Roadshow* while she cooked dinner. Thursdays were her night to cook, and she always made pasta with tomato sauce and melted goat cheese and red pepper flakes, something she'd invented one night by throwing random things in the saucepan.

"Honey, they have a lamp just like that horrid one at Elsa's. Come look!"

Maggie delivered steaming plates of pasta perched on wooden trays to her parents, and watched the announcer give the value of the lamp. The lamp's owner looked duly surprised, delighted, and humbled. Maggie's mom and dad were engrossed as they dug into their food, muttering things like "Can you imagine?" and "Payday." Sometimes she envied her parents, the way they were so streamlined with each other, how they watched the same shows every night and how a lot of things—though obviously not all—seemed settled for them, instead of so unpredictable as it was for her.

After she ate, she climbed the creaky stairs, changed into her boxers and tank top, and crawled into bed, her room toasty and cozy because of the big radiator near the foot of her bed. She turned out the lights but couldn't sleep. Faintly she could hear Abe barking across the field. He'd taken up the habit, in the last few days, of barking at the woods.

Maggie woke sometime later, thinking she was dreaming the howling, but it was Abe again, howling at the top of his lungs. She looked at the clock; it was almost three. She noticed an orange flicker through the trees out the window. She stood from bed, half asleep, and leaned against the glass to get a better look, her forehead turning cold. There was a strange illumination deep in the woods, flaring and retreating over and over.

"Fire," she whispered.

It was in the woods where Liam's house had to be.

"Mom." She shook her mom awake moments later, after she'd pulled on her flannel pants. "I think there's a fire at Liam's."

Her parents were awake and groggily pulling themselves out of bed when she took off, throwing on a sweater and her boots, pulling a blanket around her arms and running out into the snow. Hearing panting, she realized Abe was at her side just as she reached the clearing.

It was the roof. Half the roof was up in flames.

A shadow was running back and forth across the lawn, and she saw to her relief that it was Liam.

"The lake," he breathed, thrusting a bucket into her arms. "We broke the ice; get water from the lake." The fire licked up the sides of the house and flared along the roof. Liam's dad appeared from around a corner with another bucket, and they began to work, coughing because of the thick, black smoke as they tried to keep the fire under control. Wherever the water hit, it seemed to chase the flames to another part of the house's frame.

The icicles hanging from the corners of the roof evaporated before their eyes. Then pieces of the roof began to disintegrate and fall in. The beautiful cupola blackened and burned and fell inward. Her dad was behind her when she looked and said her mom was on the phone with 911, though Mr. Witte had already called them.

By the time the fire trucks arrived, the roof of the Wittes' living room was gone. Liam and his dad stood back, panting and wiping soot from their faces, trying to get breaths of fresh air.

A light snow had begun to fall, and Maggie thought that might help slow the flames. And then a long, thick stream of water hit from the direction of the first fire truck. The fire began to shrink and die quickly under the power of the fire hoses.

They watched as the flames sputtered and died. It took several long, agonizing minutes, but it was much faster than Maggie would have imagined.

She didn't see the letters in the yard until a little while later, when she was crossing to get a blanket from the fire truck to wrap around Liam's dad.

MURDERER, it said in black stones, stretching across the snowy yard. And then a pitchfork, also made of stones.

She tried to kick it away before Liam caught sight of it, but looking up, she saw him standing with his hands against his hips, watching her—looking not shocked, only tired.

After they'd talked to the police and her parents had straggled home, making Maggie promise she'd follow them soon, Liam and Maggie went down to the lake, and Liam chipped at the edge of the newly, thinly refrozen ice until he reached the water. He washed most of the soot off his face, but it still clung to the edges along his hairline.

"Come here," he said, and he took his shirt, dipped it in the water, and rubbed it against Maggie's face—her cheeks, her forehead, her chin. Then he surveyed her. "You still look like you crawled through a chimney, but it's better."

"Do I look like Santa?" she asked, trying to cheer him up, and he smiled, but then looked like he might break down and cry, and Maggie wiped some of the soot off his face with the inside of her sleeve.

They were still huddled together at the edge of the lake when darkness began to give way to morning, and the sun began to show what was left of Liam's roof.

"It could have been much worse," he said. "It's only the roof."

"And everything's wet," Maggie said. For some reason she thought of Liam's beautiful light show. The ceiling where they'd watched it was gone.

When they returned Mr. Witte was talking to the police,

and someone was helping him make a reservation to stay at a local hotel.

"We'll go to the hotel once we're done here," Liam said as they stood at the edge of the driveway saying good-bye. "I'll call you."

One of the women in a four-wheel-drive emergency vehicle offered to drop off Maggie. She badly wanted to stay and help, but she didn't know what she could do. She climbed into the car and watched through the rear window as Liam and his dad stood in the yard looking helpless.

Hurrying up her own driveway in the dim dawn light, she let herself inside soundlessly. Once in the bathroom, she scrubbed her body, threw her soot-stained clothes in the hamper, put on a thin tank top, and got into bed, pulling her fluffy, warm comforter around her like a shield, relief to be home and safe flooding her, but mingled with a heavy sadness. She fell asleep to the chirping of the birds. And then she woke to the sound of someone in her room. She remembered she had forgotten to lock the front door. She could hear the breathing before she opened her eyes.

It was Liam. He put his finger in front of his mouth and knelt by the side of her bed. "I just wanted to say thank you. I forgot to," he said. "I'm sorry." He looked deeply sad, a little fragile, and so tired.

"No . . ." She sat up. "*I'm* sorry, Liam. I am so, so sorry."

He shook his head. He was staring at her mouth, and he began to sit back on his heels, pulling away, when Maggie leaned forward and put her hand on his shoulder. Gently, scared he would stand up, she stroked his collarbone, something she'd thought of doing a million times, just to see what it felt like.

He reached for her, clasped the lower part of her back, and pushed his mouth against hers. His hands were in her hair and then pulling her closer, as if she couldn't be close enough. Then he abruptly stopped. He put his forehead against hers and looked in her eyes.

"Sorry," he said.

"But . . ."

He stood up, turned, crossed the room in what seemed like two steps, and was gone.

15

THINGS WERE QUIET IN GILL CREEK, AND ALL OVER THE PENINSULA PEOPLE waited with bated breath for the other shoe to drop. The more days that went by without incident, it seemed to Maggie, the more people were on their guard. Even at the grocery store, shoppers and tellers seemed less friendly and easy.

Liam didn't come back to Water Street for the next few days, and he didn't call. Maggie tried to get it out of her system; she ran every day, despite the cold; she threw herself into schoolwork. *He'd* kissed *her*. If it had been a mistake, it had been his mistake. She didn't need to feel embarrassed about it. What embarrassed her was how much she thought of the kiss, like she couldn't control her brain. She wasn't as scared of him saying he'd made a mistake, and how much it would wound her pride, as she was of not getting to feel that feeling again, that hungry, wild giddiness.

She decided to try to work on her mural again, the one she'd tried to start when she moved in. She had an idea for it. Moths, fluttering around a moon. It would take lots of dark blue for the night sky and grays and pale, pale reds for just a hint of color shading the moths' wings. She began to sketch it, envisioning the colors vividly as she penciled in the outlines.

She jumped at a *thunk* at her window and looked up to see the dripping remnants of a snowball sliding down the glass. She looked outside. Liam stood in the yard. He lifted a hand out of his pocket and held it up toward her in a wave.

Maggie swallowed the lump in her throat and went downstairs slowly, pulling on her boots at the edge of the kitchen, then opening the front door. He was already climbing the stairs. She stepped out, closed the door behind her, and leaned back against it, unsure. They looked at each other awkwardly, and then Maggie moved to the left, shivering, to make room for him on the landing, and he moved to the left at the same time. Uncertainly he put both his hands on either side of her face. "You're cold?" She nodded, and mid-nod he kissed her, his lips trembling slightly. Then he pulled back. He looked at her seriously but hopefully.

"I'm a lot more nervous now. Last time I was running on adrenaline."

Maggie couldn't get her voice to work. She reached for the lapel of his coat and held tight to it, feeling her face heat up.

He reached around her and pushed her back against the railing and kissed her much harder, running his hands down her lower back. Finally she pushed him away, dizzy. "My dad's home."

Liam took two steps back like he'd touched something hot, and they stared at each other. "Sorry." He shook his head. "I just . . . looking at you . . ."

"Wanna come in? Officially meet my dad?"

Liam nodded, out of breath. "Sure. Sure. I'd love to meet him. I mean, since my house isn't on fire this time."

Maggie's dad was at the kitchen table over his home-repair book, where possibly he'd seen everything.

"Dad, this is Liam."

"Hi, Liam. I prefer that if you want to make out with my daughter, you do it where I can't see it? I'm old-fashioned that way."

A red flush crawled up Liam's face. "Yeah, yeah, of course, I'm so sorry, Mr. Larsen. I will . . . I mean, we wouldn't . . ."

Maggie's dad fake-yawned, as if to say he wanted to drop the subject.

"I think we might go for a walk or something," Maggie said.

Her dad raised his eyebrows at them. "Bring your pepper spray."

They stepped out into the blinding-white day and cracked up when they got halfway across the yard.

"I thought you might never come back," Maggie said.

Liam looked at her, amazed. "Crazy." And then he hoisted her into the air and over his shoulder and carried her across the snow. And even though Maggie had never been much of a squealer, she squealed and let him carry her as far as he wanted.

Pauline,

Things are pretty flat here. Scary as usual. Glad you are in killer-free Milwaukee, though I miss you a ton. Elsa says we (our thriving metropolis of Gill Creek) are going to be featured on 60 Minutes next week. They're interviewing the police chief and of course Hairica. Elsa is always the first to know these things.

Liam finished the sauna. The only thing missing is you.

Love, Maggie

A week after Liam had shown up on her porch, Maggie sat over a letter to Pauline. She told herself she was only partially obscuring the truth. She did miss Pauline. But nothing, in those middle days of January, was flat. Not the rise and fall of her breath when she saw Liam walking across the snowy side yard or the spiking and slamming of her pulse when he pulled her against a tree to kiss her on their long rambles through the woods or the way her heart spiked when she opened her door to find something he'd left her on the porch: a book on caterpillars or a pair of binoculars or a pinecone.

Maggie felt like she'd put herself knowingly in danger for the first time in her life, and it was scary and exhilarating. She wanted to talk to someone about it—her mom or Elsa or Jacie, but she didn't know how to put something so overwhelming into words. Her dad was the person she usually talked to about big things, but talking to him about Liam would make her feel awkward and squidgy. Invisible as it might be to everyone else, she felt like she'd jumped a gap.

She put the letter in an envelope, addressed and stamped it, then sat staring out her window. At a loss, she stood and went to her shelves, found her old sketchbook, and sat again, studying the pictures one by one. She'd done them ages ago when she still drew: sketches of her mom rolling out bread dough, her apartment building in Chicago, butterflies in the park they used to go to. She'd filled the outlines in with pastels; that had always been her favorite part. The drawings were mostly gray pencil with flashes of color on cheeks or wings or eyes.

Biting her lip thoughtfully, she dug out her old charcoals and pastels and opened to an empty page. She started drawing the Boden house across the lawn, giving the windows the warm light that let you know there was life going on inside. Sketching things like this had always taken her somewhere else—to a version of life that was vivid and where everything meant "something," even inanimate objects. She wanted to make the house reflect the personality of its residents. She remembered when she'd been little, she'd been able to sit and draw for hours at a time. Was it too late to go back to that feeling? After a few false starts in which she couldn't get the warmth of the windows quite right, she let out a frustrated sigh. No matter how hard she tried, the angles were wrong, the house looked lifeless, and the colors she'd picked and blended didn't fit.

"I'm too rusty," she said to no one.

She tried a couple more strokes, getting nowhere, then closed the sketchbook and put it back on its shelf.

I'll try again tomorrow, she thought. *Maybe Liam will let me sketch him, for practice.*

She did come back to it the next night and the night after that. Sometimes she tried to draw Liam. But always, when she did, the person who ended up flying from her pencil—with the scar down her back and the spaced-out teeth and the lit-up eyes—was Pauline.

It was amazing how quickly a roof could be rebuilt, though it was a slipshod one and needed to be shingled. Liam and his dad had moved out all their waterlogged things and pulled up the rugs. Insurance was paying for a lot, but as born do-it-yourselfers, they were reflooring the living room themselves. Liam's room was livable, and his dad had moved down to what had been a spare room at the other end of the house until his room was ready. It was a little drafty but not too uncomfortable. The insulation had gone in almost immediately after the roof.

Maggie snuck out the first night they were back, surprising him by tapping on his window. She crawled in, and he pulled her under the covers with him and covered her in kisses, on her lips, her cheeks, her neck, her forehead— breathing her in, in his sleepy, half-awake but very turned-on way. He touched her as if he were afraid of offending her or invading her space, just very lightly on her arms, her neck, shyly, his hands slightly trembling like he was trying to keep himself in check. Maggie was less gentle toward him and was embarrassed by how much she wanted to touch as much of him as possible. He threaded his fingers through hers tightly. "I never saw this coming," he kept saying.

They didn't talk about Pauline. Her name was conspicuously missing from their hours together. Maggie didn't even have room in her head for Pauline. She was threaded as taut as a wire; her thoughts were scattered and her blood ran hot; even running didn't help on the days when the road was clear enough to do it.

She couldn't burn the energy out of her veins. And Liam, apparently, felt the same way. Often he lingered in her yard with Abe even after they'd said good-bye, as if going farther and farther out of her sight was painful. He'd crouch and scratch Abe's ears, delaying, and smile up at her window before trailing off slowly through the woods or down Water Street.

But there was the sense of waiting too. There was a feeling that they were in a bubble, and Maggie had the overwhelming sense, from time to time, that it would have to pop whenever Pauline came home. But that might be months away. And it might be never.

16

MAGGIE HAD DECIDED TO SUCK IT UP AND START DOING HER OWN LAUNDRY, but she still always hurried through it because she didn't like to stay down in the cellar long. One afternoon as she was yanking the last of the warm, dry clothes from the dryer into her laundry basket, she noticed an envelope at the bottom of the stairs that led to the slanted outer door. It looked like it had been slid in under the door. She opened the envelope to find a folded note and some dried flowers.

Maggie,

You may never find this, since you never go under-ground, but I thought it might be cool to see if you did.

*I picked these daisies in the summer and stuck them in
a book. Now they're a little piece of summer for you.*

*Maggie, I don't always string words together bril-
liantly when I'm talking, but I wanted to say you are so
beautiful. Your curves and those firm legs make me light-
headed. But you're also this beautiful person. You always
think about other people. You never shout for attention,
you're a sleeper, you hold all your best stuff close to your
chest. You always seem to know where you're going. You
always seem to know exactly who you are.*

*I'm so glad I met you. I can't wait to touch you again.
Smack my mouth, but damn I have to say I like touching
you.*

Liam

Maggie traced the words with her fingers. She wondered
if he'd picked and dried the flowers thinking he'd give them
to Pauline. But she decided she didn't care, that she wouldn't
look a gift flower in the mouth. The old Maggie would have
parsed things out and gone over the possible negatives. But
not now. She blushed thinking that her mom might have
found the note instead of her.

She started to tuck it into her pocket, but instead she
decided to hide it somewhere in the basement, like her own
dragon treasure. She tucked it near the back of the room,
on a ledge, under an old piece of loose cinder block. Maybe

someone would find it one day and wonder about it, just like Liam had found the bracelet.

That afternoon they raced through the woods in their big boots, and Liam caught her around her stomach and hugged her tight against him like he'd never let go, then threw her in the snow to make her laugh. Cold and wet, they ran to the sauna and, once inside, they sat with their legs entwined and took off their shirts. Maggie felt as if she were unwrapping pieces of herself and letting him see, inside and out.

He leaned his forehead against hers. It was strange how she'd never made so much eye contact with anyone in her life, but it was endlessly interesting with him. It felt like she was coming to know exactly the numbers of lines in the coronas around his pupils. He traced her shoulders with his hands, carefully avoiding moving them anywhere else.

"I should have built this for you," he said.

"Let's pretend that you did."

Liam sat up, pulling away from her. She felt the loss of his body the moment she wasn't touching him. "Okay, let's make it official," he said. He opened the sauna door, peering around onto the ground outside, then stepped out in his bare feet.

"You're going to freeze, Crazy."

After a couple of minutes the door opened and he reappeared, happy and shivering, with a nail in his hand. "I knew I'd left a couple of these suckers in the gutter."

He shoved the door closed and, still shivering, raised his

hand above it, just under the roofline, etching something in the wood with the tip of the nail. When he stepped back, she saw he'd carved a word there: *Maggie's*.

He sank back down beside her, laying the nail in a slat of the bench.

"I wanna take you somewhere this afternoon," he said. "If we leave early, we can be back when we're supposed to."

"Sounds familiar."

Liam looked pained, and then he said, "No. It's something just for you. I've never even been there myself."

Maggie sank in tighter against him, their chests touching.

"Yes," she said. "Okay."

They left within the hour.

I step back. I give the lovers their privacy, that's the least they deserve: one moment that's just for them. For these moments of Maggie's life, her love flares up and lights up the world. It's like dropping a match into a well.

I hide in the cellar and try, instead, to imagine myself into these places.

I imagine us as friends. We laugh and run around in circles, leaving our footprints in the snow. I don't know what my footprints would look like, what size shoe I had if I ever lived, who Pauline and Liam and Maggie would have seen when they looked at me. But still I imagine we're lying on the Larsen roof, talking about all the people we know, that I am a teenager too. In my imagination there are so many people I know and love.

We could have set the world on fire too, if we'd been friends. But we never were.

I try to imagine that the three of them—or even just Pauline and Maggie—come with me into the cellar, where the bright emptiness is, the growing shaft of light. I try to imagine that they stand beside me when I finally get close. But I always get there first and too fast. And the big, empty place is there as if it's *just been waiting for me the whole time. And I'm so scared—so deeply scared with every fiber of my invisible existence—to go away.*

Then again, sometimes I worry I will never leave Door County at all.

* * *

A couple of days later, Maggie and Liam drove to the local diner for dinner in Liam's dad's car. It was dusk, and they wove along the windy road into town, watching the lights begin to come on in the houses along their route.

They kept the windows cracked despite the cold because it smelled so good, piney and fresh. Liam turned up the heat full blast, and the cold and hot mixed together. He tuned the radio to *Delilah*, and soft, cheesy music drifted into the air. He grinned at her. But Maggie was lost in thought. She wanted to say something, but she didn't know how. She thought maybe Liam Witte was her first great thing, and she wanted him to know. But then the moment passed by as he took a slow left and they pulled up to the diner.

They were just pulling into a spot when she noticed the flashing red and blue lights at the police station across Route 42. Liam parked, and they climbed out and stood with their backs against the car, staring.

Reporters had gathered in front of the main door of the station, and the parking lot was so bright with camera lights, it looked like it could be daytime. A few people had come out of the diner to watch, and one of the waitresses Maggie knew walked up beside them.

"Can you believe it?" she asked. "He works at the antiques shop. All this time. Can you believe it?"

They stared at the spectacle across the street as Gerald

Turner was led across the lot in handcuffs. Cars and TV crews were pouring into the lot, and so many flashes were going off, it felt like lightning.

That night it was on every broadcast in the county. The Door County Killer had been caught.

17.

PAULINE BODEN CAME HOME HOLDING JAMES FALK'S HAND. SHE STOOD AT Maggie's door one gray afternoon in early February like she'd never left. She lowered her chin into her bright blue Patagonia ski jacket and said that her mom had let her come home for good now that the killer had been caught.

She shoved a gift into Maggie's hand: a snow globe of Milwaukee, white snow coming down on the buildings and the river. Maggie held it in her palm, not knowing what to say.

James—tall, dark-haired, muscular—stood beside her, looking at Maggie directly and confidently. He looked exactly like the kind of guy Maggie would have pictured Pauline with when she'd first met her—very handsome and athletic, with an air of holding the world on a string. He thrust his hand into Maggie's.

"Mags. Great to meet you."

Maggie raised her eyebrows at Pauline. *Mags?* Pauline shrugged.

"I've heard a lot about you," James went on, reaching an arm around Pauline. "My girl really missed you."

"Um, yeah, I missed her too," Maggie said.

"Well, I was just dropping her home so . . ." James leaned over and kissed Pauline, pulling her in by the waist. Pauline gave the slightest resistance, let him peck her lips, and then pulled away. "I'm sure I'll be at Pauline's a lot, but don't be a stranger. The more the merrier. See you."

"Bye." They watched him walk across the yard to the driveway. Maggie wondered if he had just given her permission to hang out with her friend. Pauline turned back to her, her eyes lighting up.

"Come help me unpack."

In Pauline's room items flew from her suitcase like a hurricane. Her mom had cleaned her room while she was gone, but it was quickly disheveled as Pauline tossed clothes on the floor and toiletries across her desk. Two iPods; her portable Bose speakers; several sparkly tops; and a pair of new, bright-red platforms tumbled onto the floor, where Pauline shoved them under her bed. She talked excitedly while she threw her clothes in the pile and tossed everything else—a cracked iPad, a Tiffany heart bracelet, two purses—toward her dresser. "I'm so happy to be home. So, so happy. How are things? How's the shop? How are your parents?"

"The shop is closed. I didn't tell you? My parents are good. Everything else is"—Maggie paused, looking around the room—"the same." Maggie swallowed guiltily. "They're planning a Valentine Social thing, down at the Clipper."

"Oh, they always do that." Pauline waved her hand dismissively. She was pale and thinner even than she had been when she'd left.

Pauline noticed Maggie studying her. "I know, I look like I'm withering away. I can't take another week of winter, I'll die."

"You should try eating something other than Twizzlers."

Pauline pulled a wrinkled, balled shirt out of the suitcase, squinted at it like she'd never seen it in her life, then threw it across the room. "Yeah, I just haven't had much of an appetite. I don't know why."

Maggie nodded. "So, James seems, um, familiar with you."

"I know," she said apologetically. "It's a little intense. He's been trying to get me to go out with him forever, so I guess he's a little . . . enthusiastic. He's already saying that if I move to Milwaukee after I graduate, he will too."

"Huh." Maggie couldn't picture Pauline ever liking someone so clingy.

"He's kind of . . . intent on things. But he boxes, to get out all his energy."

"Huh."

"I know. Who boxes? But he likes it."

Pauline unpacked sweaters and boots, and at the bottom of her suitcase was a postcard. It was a piece of old Scandinavian-looking art, pencil-drawn, with a wooden Scandinavian-looking house in the background and a creepy, bony old lady hobbling along the rocks of a lakeshore. Pauline saw her studying it.

"It's from Liam," Pauline said. "It's so dumb." She held it up. "It's Pesta. Remember, the goddess of death I was telling you about? He said he saw it in a junk store and thought of me. Because he thinks I'm kind of obsessed with her." She crumpled it, then dropped it lightly into the trash can beside her dresser.

"So how does it feel that the Door County Killer gave you a gramophone?"

Maggie hated talking about it. It still felt surreal to her. She actually hadn't come around to believing it yet. She knew she should tell her parents, but the idea of laying that kind of stress down on her mom right now—just when things seemed to be coasting for the first time in years—was extremely unappealing.

They sat in silence for a while. Finally Maggie said, "Did you hear about the fire?"

Pauline nodded. "My mom told me."

"Have you gone to see him yet?"

Pauline stood up and went to her mirror and put on a wool hat she said she'd bought in Milwaukee at a winter street fair. She shook her head.

"He said you weren't writing him."

Pauline tugged the hat this way and that to position it.

"I'm glad you're back," Maggie said finally, when she didn't reply.

Pauline turned, looking uncertain for a moment. "Me too." She knelt by the bed.

"Pauline, what happened that night?" Maggie asked. "That night you got caught? Why were you out so late?" She'd never wanted to ask Liam. But now she wanted to ask Pauline.

Pauline picked at her fingernails. She looked at Maggie. "We argued," she said. Then she turned back to her suitcase. As if there were nothing more to say about it.

Maggie crept into Liam's window late that night, sneaking out after her parents had gone to bed. He woke with a start, then reflexively pulled her into his arms and kissed her, breathing into her hair.

"Pauline's back," she said, after a while, low. His room smelled like new wood from where they'd patched up the roof.

"I know." His voice was so soft as he said it, as if it was a tender thing. Maggie must have stiffened, because Liam pulled her close. "This has been the best month of my life," he whispered. "I just want you to know that, Maggie. I waited for this, and I didn't even know what I was waiting for. You don't have to worry."

Strangely she wasn't worried. Not about him. She was worried, though, about Pauline.

She could hear Liam's breath grow slow and steady next to her as he drifted back toward sleep.

"I love you, Liam Witte," she said to the ceiling, then sighed. "It turns out you're my first love." He didn't respond. He just kept breathing soft and steady against her shoulder.

Maggie felt her skin prickle with embarrassment, but then, thinking he must be asleep, she moved to climb back out of bed and sneak out the window. Just as she slipped the covers down to her legs, he tightened his hold around her in a firm grip and whispered against her neck. "I love you too, Maggie."

Elsa reopened the shop that weekend. Of course she exclaimed and howled and gave off the impression that the fact that a murderer had been working under her roof was the most awful thing that had ever happened to her and, at the same time, completely expected.

"I don't get how he did it," Maggie said. "Physically, how could he do it?"

"His wife was probably his accomplice," Elsa said.

Maggie had been shocked to see, on the news, that he even had a wife. She looked like Mrs. Claus. And sadly bewildered in front of the reporters who'd camped outside her door.

Elsa spent much of the day going through Gerald's antiques as if she thought she might find a body in the vintage metal tissue box or secreted in one of the Victrolas. Maggie stood at the cash register fighting a low, steady sense of uneasiness.

Finally Elsa returned, empty-handed. She noticed Maggie staring out the window. She stood beside her.

"You look like a sea wife," she said.

"What's a sea wife?"

"Someone who's waiting for her sailor to come home but knows the sailor may be lying at the bottom of the ocean. You look pale."

Maggie pointed out the window to the low sky. "No sun makes Maggie a pale girl."

Elsa continued to look at her expectantly.

"Pauline's home."

"Well, aren't you two thick as thieves? I'd think you'd be happy."

"She and Liam aren't talking. Isn't that weird?"

Elsa placed her hand against her heart gently and shook her head. "Oh, honey, don't get in between those two. They were destined for each other; they're like two pieces of the same fabric, different as they are. They'll live and die together, mark my words."

18

PAULINE WANTED TO SEE THE PLACE WHERE HAIRICA HAD BEEN KEPT CAPTIVE. James Falk insisted on tagging along, even though Pauline had planned it to be just her and Maggie. Maggie figured it was either because he wanted to impress Pauline with his fearlessness or because there was nothing else to do in Gill Creek this time of year.

They entered Zippy's Amusement Park through the side gate, which was crooked and half fallen down. The Ferris wheel loomed high and rusty above the park; the ground was covered in crunchy, hardened snow. Maggie had never been to an amusement park in winter; she wondered how eerie it would be at night, because already, in the middle of the day, it was making the hairs on the back of her neck stand up.

James led the way, holding Pauline by the hand, his fingers entwined with hers like he was trying to physically pull her closer to him. When he wasn't tugging her into his arms, he was gently grasping her waist or trying to put his hand on her lower back, basically touching her butt.

"We used to come here when I was little," he said. "I loved the strength game. You know, with the mallet?"

Pauline trailed along behind him like a tetherball, as if her hand and arm were foreign parts only coincidentally attached to her body. They walked past an empty cotton-candy stand and a line of game booths. A Scrambler sat under a tarp that James lifted and replaced. Coming upon the bumper-car pavilion, which was empty of cars, James pulled Pauline into the middle of the floor and spun her around a couple of times. She spun away, laughingly pulling out of James's arms.

"She's hard to pin down," he said to Maggie with a faltering smile as they walked behind Pauline. The image of bugs pinned to a board in her old sixth-grade classroom popped into Maggie's head.

"Oh, here it is!" he said. They were standing in front of a tall, thin tower with a bell at the top, a metal plate at the bottom, and a round, glass face with the words "Pathetic," "Is That All You've Got?" and "You've Got the Power!"

The mallet was still lying attached to the game. James picked it up. Pauline circled back to watch.

"It won't work," Maggie said. "It's supposed to be electric."

Not to mention, it was rusted and crooked-looking now. But James lifted the mallet and brought it down hard—so hard that the rusted metal plate flew sideways at impact. The bell rang out, echoing across the empty park.

"See?" James said. "It wasn't completely broken." He kicked the metal plate with his toe. "Well, I guess now it is." He grinned at Pauline, and Pauline gave Maggie an annoyed look.

They followed Pauline back toward a shed covered in police tape. She broke the tape and walked into it, her back against the wall, her hair smushed around her face as she leaned her head against the cold metal.

"Do you think this is where he kept her?" she asked.

"Pauline, get out of there; it's morbid," Maggie said.

Pauline stared around.

"This place should scare me, but it doesn't."

"I still think it's totally creepy that you're standing in there," Maggie said.

Suddenly there was a loud crack in the woods behind the shed, like a heavy, dead branch being stepped on. Pauline jumped. "What was that?"

James went to the back of the shed and peered into the trees. "Must have been an animal. I don't see anything."

"Okay, you're right, it's creepy in here," Pauline said. Maggie was relieved. She knew the killer was caught; logically she knew they were safe. But she couldn't wait to leave.

She reached in, clasped Pauline's hands, and pulled her out.

* * *

On the ride home, James kept fondling Pauline's hair with his right hand while driving with his left, making Maggie feel slightly nauseated. She kept her eyes out the window and tried to ignore them.

Coming down Water Street, she saw a figure halfway down the road, and her heart picked up a nervous beat.

Bundled up in a navy-blue wool coat and his wool hat, he waved a hand to greet them, and they slowed to a stop.

"Liam," Pauline said, rolling down the window. Maggie rolled hers down too, feeling her face flush. Liam's cheeks were flushed too, but from the cold. He looked at Maggie, then at Pauline. He glanced briefly at James, and the two nodded at each other. He leaned on the ledge of Maggie's window. "We finished the roof. You should come over later to see it."

Maggie was about to respond when Pauline spoke up from the front.

"Hey, Liam . . . ," she murmured. "How's it going?" Liam looked up at her, then back at Maggie as if he hadn't heard her.

"I'm sorry I haven't come by yet," Pauline blurted out.

"Not a big deal," Liam said, turning back to Maggie. "Anyway, come over later if you want." Then, he did something Maggie didn't expect, even as it was happening. He leaned forward, put his hands on either side of her face, and pulled her in for a kiss on the lips.

He smiled at her, then turned and started walking up his

driveway. Maggie swiveled back in her seat to look at Pauline, her heart lodged thickly in her throat.

Pauline was staring out at Liam, her mouth open, speechless. She had her hands rested on the dash, knuckle side down, palms open, as if asking for something or begging or as if something had been taken out of her hands.

That night Maggie saw the circle of a bonfire out at the edge of the lake. She trudged across the field and down to the water, Abe barking somewhere deep in the woods. She stood near the fire Pauline had made and held up her hands to the heat.

"Wanna sit?" Pauline asked.

Maggie squinted at her in the dark. Pauline had cleared a big patch of snow off the beach and laid a camping lamp and a bag of Cheetos on a blanket there, then squeezed her legs into a sleeping bag. "My mom is driving me nuts. I almost want to *sleep* out here." Abe came jogging up to the fire, out of breath.

Maggie sank down on the edge of the blanket, and Pauline unzipped her sleeping bag and unfolded it, covering Maggie's legs. A plane passed overhead. Abe growled at the woods, and Pauline petted his snout. The light from the windows of the Boden house winked at them through the bare branches of the trees. Maggie pulled the sleeping bag tight against her chest and scootched a little closer to the fire.

"Are you a good flier?" Pauline asked.

Maggie nodded. She'd flown a lot—to her grandmother's

in Boston, to Disney World as a kid, and once to London for a family trip, back when their finances had been better.

Pauline sighed. "I'm always scared the plane will fall out of the sky."

"I thought I was the one with phobias."

Pauline shook her head. "You're pretty brave, I think. You just think what *could* happen. You don't just rush into stuff stupidly."

Maggie knew she wasn't as brave as Pauline thought. Pauline smoothed back her long hair where it spilled out under her hat, leaning her wiry body forward against her legs for warmth. "I always change my mind. I'm flighty." Pauline looked over at her appraisingly. "You're the kind of person who does what you say you are going to do. I mean, you say it, and then you do it. I really admire that. You probably have a really great life ahead of you."

Maggie shivered and wrapped her arms around herself. "Yep, I'm perfect," she said drily, poking fun at herself. "Pauline, you have a great life ahead too." Pauline didn't look convinced. They stared out at the dark lake as Maggie worked up to an apology.

"I'm happy for you and Liam," Pauline said suddenly, running a stick through the snow, scratching back and forth, poker-faced. She shifted her weight to the left.

"Pauline, I wanted to tell you, but . . ."

"Do you love him?" she asked.

Maggie felt her face flush. She nodded.

"Oh." Pauline's voice sounded thin and frail. "That's really good. You both deserve it. I mean it."

Maggie wanted to divide herself in half. She wanted half of herself to make everything right for Pauline. And the other half wanted to go to Liam's window, float into his bed, and hear him breathe. It thrilled her a little, looking at how beautiful Pauline was, and knowing that Liam loved *her*, Maggie.

"Do you think people watch over you after they die?" Pauline asked.

"Not really," Maggie said, trying to be honest. She wasn't a VW-Bus-driving-level atheist, but she wasn't much of a believer either.

"I do. I think you go on. I don't think you disappear. I think my dad watches over me, like my guardian angel. Only sometimes I feel like if I leave here, or if I change too much, he won't come with me, and he won't recognize me anymore."

Maggie didn't know what to say.

They sat awhile longer, but it felt like there was nothing more really to say, at least not tonight. Finally Maggie stood and brushed off her jeans under her coat. She left Pauline and Abe sitting there by the lake, still wide-awake and looking for planes.

Back inside, her mom had the news on again. Maggie was just thinking that she'd never known her mom to be such a TV hound when she turned through the archway and saw the screen.

"Can you believe it?" her mom was whispering.

On the screen was a live shot of Gerald Turner, giving a press conference, having just been released from custody on lack of evidence.

Maggie's first thought was that she wished they hadn't gone to Zippy's. It felt, now, like they'd been waking the dead.

Over the amusement park, I watch the watcher.

He's come back looking for something, and he's seen them. His eyes are stuck to Pauline, sticky as flypaper.

He's a shadow; a bulky, bad man. He keeps his face down as if he knows even God is watching. He is collecting up his things and planning his next steps, and I can only watch him like a movie.

I know that I've come to love these people beneath me when the sight of him gets my soul shaking and the moths scattering. They return, but their tiny shapes shiver with my anger.

The cellar pulls me toward home.

Everywhere, recently, I see glimpses of other spirits, peeking out from behind bushes, giving off a faint light from under porches, glowing mournful faces as they stare out of dark windows or sit by old graves, waiting. It's like they let me see them now, as if I'm becoming one of them. I don't know what any of them are here to do, but I think maybe at the end of it they'll each go through their own terrifying bright holes, just like I will.

I check on the teenagers on Water Street, asleep in their beds:

Liam, with an arm slung under his head, a vague

smile on his lips because he's thinking about a girl. Maggie, curled tight in her comforter, knowing she's the girl he thinks about. And Pauline.

Pauline is lying on her right side, Abe tucked in a ball against her belly. She's holding something in her right fist, crumpled up and tight, close to her cheek. A postcard of Pesta.

19

MID-FEBRUARY. THE GILL CREEK VALENTINE SOCIAL WAS HELD AT THE Clipper, a sweeping, white Victorian hotel with a wrap-around porch hovering above a green lawn that raced down to the lake. Maggie had driven past the hotel before but had never been inside, though Liam sometimes worked there for his catering job. He'd said he might be assigned there tonight, and if he was, he'd sneak out to see her.

As she and Pauline and James crossed the parking lot, clouds slid across the sky, the sun going dim and bright again. It was heavy-coat weather but not freeze-your-nose-hairs frigid. The warmish front was supposed to last for a couple of days. The weather had turned strange: layer upon layer of clouds moving slowly inland, white puffs piled on lighter gray piled on blue.

"We may get one of those crazy midwinter thunderstorms," James said. He knew a lot about the weather. Pauline said he got As in everything.

Inside, they peeled out of their coats. Pauline was wearing a dress she'd bought online from Barneys in New York—eggshell white and thin and drapey, with one strap on her left shoulder and the other shoulder bare. She wore a comb with tufty, delicate, tiny feathers in her dark hair. Everyone else looked overdone compared to her. The thin dress was barely visible on her shivering frame; it contradicted the elaborate corsage James had slipped on her wrist.

Maggie's own dress was one she'd had for two years: emerald green, simple, and structured. She'd worn it last year to a dance in Chicago, on a date with a guy who'd bored her the whole night, saying things like "Really? *Really?*" over and over again, thinking it was clever. She'd drunk three disgusting swigs out of the flask of cheap whiskey he'd brought in his coat just to power through the ennui.

The Gill Creek dance had been pushed into one of the three main ballrooms, which was packed. It was an Under the Sea theme; there were blue and white balloons arranged along the ceiling to look like waves and buxom, retro paper mermaids pasted to the walls and fake starfish and shells dotting the refreshments table.

"I suspect these mermaids have been surgically enhanced," Maggie said.

"No, I'm pretty sure 39-18-32 is a totally realistic measurement for mermaids," Pauline offered sarcastically.

"I don't think they have pelvises. Oh, we women and our huge, unattractive, structurally necessary pelvises."

The room was stuffy, and the dancing had already started. Maggie felt her face flushing with heat. James took their coats and told them he'd grab them some food and drinks. He wore a slim suit and, Maggie thought as she watched him, he moved like this was his place, like every place was his place.

"It's nice to have five minutes when he's not trying to touch my ass," Pauline said, sighing forlornly and watching him. "You should see it when we're alone. It's like kissing the giant squid; he tries to get everywhere at once."

"You should break up with him if you don't like him," Maggie said.

"I know, I know." Pauline looked at her. "I'm kind of just . . . coasting. He makes everything easy."

James came back with plates full of food, and Pauline devoured hers. "Dance?" he asked. Some of his friends were dancing in a group at the right of the dance floor.

Pauline shook her head. "I feel a little hot actually."

"Wanna leave?" He looked a bit overly concerned, as if she were a baby or a delicate flower.

Pauline shook her head again. "No, that's okay. I'm just gonna go walk a little and see the rest of the hotel. I'll be back. You guys stay and hang out." She took off down a plush, carpeted hallway to the left.

Maggie and James stood in silence, Maggie feeling awkward because she had nothing to say to him. "My Humps" came on, which made it even a little more awkward when a couple in front of them started grinding.

"So you and Liam," James said, after a while.

"Uh-huh," Maggie replied. What else was there to say to that?

"Wasn't he into Pauline for a while?"

"Probably not something you ask someone's girlfriend."

"So you're his girlfriend?" James pressed.

Maggie wasn't sure what to say to that. She could feel herself flushing with annoyance at having her personal life invaded. "Oh, that's right. Pauline says you don't like to reveal very much. She says you hold back." Maggie tried to ignore the slight hurt that Pauline had said something like that about her.

James smiled, seeming completely at ease. "I can tell you don't like me." Maggie looked up at him but didn't argue. "Sorry to be pushy. I just don't think Pauline always knows what's best for her. I just don't think Liam Witte is what's best for her, even as a friend. That dude is seriously messed up. Sorry."

"You'd make a really good Taliban boyfriend," Maggie said. James smirked and rolled his eyes.

"She's just so beautiful," he finally said. "I've been obsessed with her since, like, seventh grade. I mean, half the guys in my class are. She makes the other girls at our school look like nothing. If you have any hints about . . . I dunno, how I can win her over . . ."

"I gotta pee," Maggie said, turning abruptly for the hall.

She was so annoyed and so over the conversation, she didn't notice a figure at the corner of her eye coming out into the hallway through the double doors that led to the kitchen. The figure crossed the back of the room with two trays, taking a shortcut to a convention room across the hotel. Only as it disappeared out the rear glass doors did she register that it was someone she knew.

Here is a moment that sparkles hard like a diamond.

Pauline Boden walks out into the plush, green-carpeted hotel lobby, then out onto the empty veranda in back and crosses to the railing. Leaning over the side, she shivers in her eggshell dress but doesn't go inside. She watches the clouds roll along and reflect in the water and rubs her arms. A squirrel scurries up a tree across the lawn, and there is the faint echo of music coming from one of the weddings inside.

Suddenly, hearing footsteps coming across the deck, she turns. Liam stands there looking uncertain, paused with two empty trays in his hands, frozen in place. He puts them down.

Pauline opens her mouth to say something, but instead, on impulse, she takes a step toward him. She puts her hands on his shoulders, and he winces.

She leads them into a dance in time to the faint music, polka steps, but slow and easy. Liam, unsure, puts a hand on her waist. He looks lost. He watches her in confusion. His fingers tremble a little on her waist.

The sun is setting and filtering through the strange clouds, and it makes the sky seem closer, like if they swam off the edge of the porch, they could reach it in twenty strokes or so. Liam pulls back and looks at her.

"You never wrote me," he says. "You're supposed to be my friend."

Pauline shakes her head sadly. "I'm not your friend."

Her lips tremble. She looks like she wants to cry.

Liam doesn't ask her why. Maybe he knows. He smooths a piece of hair back behind her ear nervously, as if she might slap his hand away.

"I'm sorry," she says.

Liam looks down at his feet.

"I'm tired of doing this," she says. "If I lose you . . . if you lose me . . ." She rolls her eyes up at the sky, tears welling along her bottom lashes. "It's so tiring trying not to love you, Liam." She looks uncertain, scared that the words are out.

Clouds cross the sun like a warning. Liam looks at Pauline's trembling lips for a while, and then she startles him, sliding forward and pressing her lips against his. He pulls away, looks angry. But after a moment, he pulls her in tight and kisses her back. They lean into each other as if they've been on a long journey, as if they're exhausted.

The moment feels familiar, like I already knew, and yet it comes as a surprise.

Now, at the back of the porch, I see her, looking

through one of the dark glass doors of the hotel. The air shifts, shudders—I feel the past rearing up at me, and then it slips away. Only it leaves a residue of something . . . a piece of myself I'm scared to know. I'm terrified, for a moment, that I've done something terrible, but I can't remember what.

From beyond the glass, Maggie Larsen watches them kiss, looking like she could sink beneath the ground.

I turn away, agitated. I float out above the woods. Despite not breathing, I need the air.

And here, I find them. Deep in the pine woods, above the trees, I arrive at the ball of ghosts. They're twirling in the air, iridescent, glowing, windblown.

The ghosts of Door County are making the lightning dance. By trying to dance with one another.

I float to a woman with a long, thin face, but my words fall on deaf ears, and her mouth moves with no sound.

I fly to a man with a crooked neck. He barely looks at me.

And finally I realize what I have for a while suspected. We ghosts aren't living among one another at all. We must be written on different slices of time or pieces of air. We'll never touch, and we'll never talk.

We're all alone.

The moths dance around us, almost like they're their own circle of moonlight.

It's a crescendo. It's tragic. Because I know what it means. It means we are—I am—a piece of the past. And I can't save anyone on Water Street.

It means I'm only here to watch.

I drift out and away again. I turn my face away from the world.

This is no place for anyone with a heart.

20

A WHITE WIND SWEPT THE SNOW IN LATE THAT FEBRUARY. IT COVERED DOOR County like a blanket, as if it wanted to lay a sheet over the horror. Another girl dead, and the peninsula had turned inward for the rest of the winter. Adults stayed indoors or retreated to wood-paneled bars to sit by roaring fireplaces. The young people sought each other out at one another's houses or occasionally snuck out to stand huddled in the snow and talk with their breath puffing out in the air, daring the darkness. This was the time of year when it felt like maybe time wasn't moving and the whole world would be stuck below freezing forever. It was like the earth was no longer in orbit but only hovering somewhere far from the sun.

Maggie hadn't told Pauline what she'd seen. But the fact that everything had changed had been unspoken among the three of them on the way home from the dance—the silence in the car, the tension when they'd all parted in the driveway, James and Pauline going one way and Maggie the other. She and Pauline hadn't talked since. Maggie hadn't returned her calls and hid when there was a knock at the door, telling her parents to say she wasn't home.

But she could sit up in her window, watching it all: Pauline and James arguing in the yard, and James finally driving away. Pauline in the passenger seat of her Subaru while Liam drove, probably riding to the diner so they could sit for hours leaning across the table toward each other, hands darting together and apart. The shaft of light across the yard as Pauline snuck out to meet Liam after curfew. Pauline leaving her window cracked open all night, letting in the cold air and waiting till the rocks hit her screen announcing his arrival. It was hard to watch, and it was hard not to.

On a normal year in Door County, Elsa said, February could break your heart. You were into the season as deep as you would ever be out of it, and it seemed that all signs of life, any sign that summer had ever existed or would ever exist again, had vanished. The sky lay low over Lake Michigan, and there were no surprises, no new faces downtown. Everything—the days themselves—only moved ahead, one foot in front of the other. And Elsa was right. The days looked the same each morning when Maggie woke up.

The snow had piled up too deep for her to run at all. She spent a lot of time wandering the house and the yard, because there was nowhere else to go and only so much schoolwork to keep her occupied. Elsa gave her a pair of used snowshoes that had come into the antiques store—which she miraculously hadn't reclosed yet, and which Gerald Turner had returned to, without a word to anyone about what had happened. (He'd just walked back in one morning and resumed his regular routine.) Maggie tromped around the woods in the shoes, but only on the side farthest from Pauline's. Back home, she would have been happy to read, but this was one thing Pauline had changed in her life: She no longer loved to just sit still. It made her feel, now, like she was missing something.

She bought a book on birds and tried to track and identify all the birds in the woods around her house. And she threw herself into finishing up the interior of the house. She sanded the banisters and helped her dad stain the floors that hadn't been done yet. Together they repainted the upstairs hallways and replaced the cabinets in the kitchen with cabinets her dad had gotten on sale at a reclaimed home-goods store in Green Bay. Day after day, the final pieces of their house came together.

She hid in the back rooms when Pauline knocked on the door. Only Abe was a regular visitor. Now that Pauline was back, he was confused about who to protect, and he spent most of the days jogging back between the Larsens' and the

Bodens' to check on both houses and make sure everything was secure.

Maggie tried to put everything else out of her mind. She retreated inside herself like she'd done in the past—when her mom had lost her job, when they'd had the car accident long before that.

But she couldn't forget. She couldn't forget Liam's hands on her skin or his breath in her hair or how it had felt like her whole body was filled with thudding drumbeats when he touched her.

"Wounds make you deeper and bigger," her dad said, one night in front of the fire, even though she hadn't told him what had happened. "The bigger the challenges you face, the bigger and deeper your soul gets." Maggie smiled at him as if the words were encouraging. But she felt the opposite: like her heart had turned small and hard. It surprised her that she couldn't stop the ache in her chest. At night she gazed at the ceiling and obsessed over whether Liam kissed Pauline exactly like *they'd* kissed. She tried to think of other things, like reciting the alphabet backward, but inevitably she was bleary-eyed each morning when she came down to the kitchen, and her mom looked at her across the table in concern.

One of these mornings, while Maggie was looking for one of her snowshoes, which had somehow wandered off from its mate, her mom announced that she had an interview in Chicago. Maggie turned to her in shock and sat back on her heels from where she'd been kneeling to reach under the couch. Her whole body lit up.

"You mean, we'd move home?" she asked, disbelieving.

Mrs. Larsen shrugged. "If I got it. I don't know how many people they're interviewing. Don't get your hopes up yet."

But Maggie's heart beat rapidly. It seemed like a perfectly timed escape. She could put Pauline and Liam and the fear that had bloomed all over Door County behind her, go back to Jacie, the familiar streets, her old, comfy, safe life. She smiled for the first time in days and, ensuring the snowshoe was nowhere to be seen under the couch, walked down the hall toward the last place it might be.

She opened the door and walked down into the musty cellar. The one ceiling bulb cast only a dim circle of light, leaving shadows in the corners of the room. Maggie looked under the stairs, moving a few boxes around before giving up, and then stood for a moment, listening. She tried to decide whether the silence was an empty one or a waiting one. She tried to imagine the life of the house before her and wondered if it had been easier then, like Pauline believed. Maggie glanced at where she'd hidden her letter under the cinder block and decided she'd leave it there forever.

Pauline was waiting in the hallway when she got to the top of the stairs.

"I tricked my way in."

Pauline had a handful of pine branches wrapped in a red

ribbon and shoved it into her hands. Her cheeks were bright pink, and her coat wasn't zipped. She was glowing, but her heart looked to be in her mouth.

"Please accept this expensive bouquet as a peace offering."

Maggie took the bouquet and laid it on the step.

Pauline looked nervous enough to vomit.

"They're doing an all-night movie lock-in thing at the Avalon next week, for all the young people. A chaperoned kind of thing. Old movies. *Snow White and . . .*" Pauline trailed off. "I was wondering . . ."

Maggie stared at her.

"Hit me. Yell at me. Something. Anything."

Maggie felt herself burn like a cool flame. She covered the icy anger that swelled up with an expressionless face. She looked at Pauline flatly, like she didn't know her. Her hands trembled, but she steadied them on the banister so Pauline wouldn't see.

A tear dribbled down Pauline's left cheek. "I know it's crazy. I know what I always said. About how I felt about him."

Maggie just went on looking at her coldly.

"Say something. Don't you care?" Pauline, who wore everything on her sleeve, couldn't recognize that some people had feelings that were deep and as still as glass.

Maggie led her down the hall, through the kitchen, and opened the door for her.

Pauline bit her lip, another tear squeezing out. A moment later she was walking off into the snow, Abe running behind her. Maggie could swear two birds circled her head and then flitted off. Like goddamned Snow White herself.

21

ASIDE FROM THE OCCASIONAL GIANT BILLBOARD FOR HOTELS OR SUBWAY OR cheese curds, the highway was flat and featureless on the drive to Chicago. Slowly buildings and then the city rose up ahead of them and replaced the humble pines of Door County with the towering buildings of the Gold Coast section of town where Maggie had grown up.

Climbing out of the car in front of her old, redbrick, eighteen-story apartment building, the first thing that struck Maggie was how loud it all was. Cars zoomed past, and two lots away a new building was going up, complete with the sound of jackhammers and bulldozers breaking concrete and beeping in reverse.

"See you tonight," her mom said, before pulling away. Her

interview was in a little over an hour. Maggie turned and faced her building again. She hadn't expected to feel so nervous and giddy at the same time.

The hallway and the elevator seemed smaller than she'd remembered; everything seemed to have shrunk in the months since she'd left, like she was Alice in Wonderland. She pushed floor five and waited.

At the end of the hall on the fifth floor, she knocked. The door opened, and a familiar face beamed at her.

"Jacie," she breathed. The two girls sank into a hug.

She and Jacie spent the first hour catching up on what had been happening with their old friends: breakups, arguments, one or two new people who'd moved into the building. Jacie was animated as she related the latest news.

It struck Maggie with a shock that, really, it had been only six months since she'd left, and nothing had changed all that much in Chicago: The same people were dating, the same people were fighting, and everyone was doing the same things on the weekends and after school.

"You have to come back," Jacie said. She'd lightened her curly, dirty-blond hair, gotten a tiny bit heavier. "I miss coffee at Meredith's and shopping at North Bridge. We could watch *Housewives* again." Maggie had secretly hated *Housewives*, but Jacie loved it. It had always been weird to her that Jacie loved to see people fight on TV.

Still, she felt weirdly floaty while they talked. All the time she'd been getting to know Pauline and Liam and the isolated beauty of her little peninsula, Jacie—and probably most of her friends—had been mostly steady, in a holding pattern. Suddenly, for the first time, Maggie felt happy that she'd left and—at the same time—a gnawing sense of loss.

"Are you scared to go to sleep at night?" Jacie asked. "With everything going on, I bet you're freaked out." Jacie was the same old Jacie: full of questions, bubbly and uncomplicated, rarely worried about too much. Even the killer seemed like a salacious detail to her.

Maggie nodded. "Kind of. I don't know. I guess I just think it couldn't happen to me. I think there's some philosophical name for that."

"You're the main character of your life," Jacie said. "You're too important to die. That's how everybody feels."

"Yeah, I'm too important to not be invincible," Maggie said.

"Delusions of grandeur," Jacie added. Before Maggie had started homeschool, they'd taken Psych together, along with a million other things. It was a tiny jab, but Maggie didn't feel the way she'd used to about Jacie's tiny jabs—like they were a necessary part of any friendship. She knew, now, that things could be better than that.

Her mom came to get her about an hour and a half later. Maggie knew Gill Creek was only a few hours away, but saying good-bye made her feel like she was returning to the ends of the earth. Jacie got teary-eyed, and they made their good-bye quick.

She and her mom drove for about an hour in silence, neither of them even turning on the radio, both lost in their thoughts.

"How was the interview?" Maggie finally asked.

"Good." Her mom nodded. "Good, good. I think I'll get a callback."

"That's great, Mom."

Maggie looked out the window, her mind moving this way and that. "Mom?"

"Yeah, Mags."

"How do you know when you give too much or too little to someone else?" she asked tentatively. "Like, how do you figure out how to love people, but then, not get . . . you know . . . walked on? How do people figure that out?"

Her mom thought for a while. "I think there probably aren't many people who have it figured out perfectly. I guess it's just little increments, always correcting this way or the other, like a seesaw. I don't know if there's any perfect balance between standing up for yourself and being generous. Although your dad sees it differently. He doesn't measure things like we do. He lives by that Saint Augustine quote: 'Love, and do what thou wilt.' He's a hippie."

"I don't think Saint Augustine was exactly a hippie," Maggie said.

"Well, you've always been smarter than me." Her mom glanced over at her, like she had a lot on her mind but was choosing her words carefully. "Mags, I do know that guys come and go when you're young. But your friends . . . those are the people who stay." It sounded to Maggie like stock parent advice—distant and cliché. Maybe her mom knew this, because she went on. "Honey . . . I know you're upset. Something with Pauline and you and Liam." Maggie picked at the upholstery under the window. Her mom always seemed to know everything Maggie didn't tell her; it was one of her gifts, like her green thumb and her knack for charming strangers and her head for numbers. "And you're trying to just hold it in and get over it on your own. But if you don't let it out . . . it'll keep growing. Things you bottle up can get bigger than you. *Talk* to Pauline. Get angry, that's fine, but just let it out."

Maggie thought about it on the way home while her mom played eighties soft-rock music on the radio.

When they climbed out of the car in the driveway that night, Maggie lingered while her mom went in. She took in the yard and her house. It looked beautiful and warmly lit and cozy, nothing like what they had started with. They'd taken something difficult and made a life out of it. Maggie realized how far they'd come, how much the house had become hers. She understood why, when she had been talking to Jacie, she'd felt like she'd lost something. She didn't belong there anymore. She belonged here.

Instead of continuing into the house, she turned and crossed the thick, wide, white field to Pauline's front door.

22

MAGGIE KNEW SHE SHOULDN'T BE THE ONE WHO WAS NERVOUS, SO SHE TRIED TO
look like she wasn't. Pauline drove, Maggie sat up in the front
seat, and Liam in the back. They barely had to look at one
another on the way to the theater, and Maggie held her chin
high as she watched the trees pass the window. Her anger
seethed under the surface, but she tried to be nice; she'd said
hi when he'd gotten into the car as if it were no big deal. She
willed herself to have a good night; she didn't want to think
she'd made a mistake in coming. She wanted to be ready to
do this and be past it.

Her mom had said, when she'd told her they were going,
that superhuman emotional strength hadn't exactly been
what she'd had in mind when they'd talked. "But you're

determined," she said, taking in Maggie's face. "You're a determined girl." And Maggie was.

Inside, not content to sit with the rabble downstairs, Pauline immediately found a back staircase to the balcony, which was off-limits. Once settled in above, they sat peering down on the crowded lower tier, watching people they knew and others from nearby towns trickling in. James Falk and some of his friends settled into one of the middle rows, and Maggie was thankful they didn't look up.

Pauline almost sparkled with the nervousness of the three of them being together but, also, happiness she couldn't hide. Maggie's chest felt like there were hot coals in her rib cage. She tried to douse it with Sprite.

Her mom had told her to let herself get angry at Pauline, but she hadn't. It had felt too much like putting her soul out even further to get pummeled. So instead she'd told her that she wanted to forget. And so that was what they were all trying to do. They were going to collectively forget that anything had ever happened between Maggie and Liam. Pauline and Liam had ended up together, just like all the experts had predicted, and they were all going to live with that. A movie was a good place to start, it seemed, because they barely had to talk.

Around 2:00 a.m., in the intermission between the third and fourth movies, the three snuck out onto the wide fire escape and sat dangling their legs over the edge, their puffy coats making their shadows against the brick back wall of the theater look like abominable snowmen. They watched the empty street below, so quiet with everything else in the town shut down.

"How's James taking the breakup?" Maggie asked, trying to think of something to talk about to distract herself. Her voice sounded distant, like small talk, as if Liam and Pauline were strangers.

"He says he's going to beat up Liam." Pauline rolled her eyes. "He's called my house a few times; it's like he thinks he owned me or something. You know, he's not such a perfect guy like everyone thinks he is. He has a temper."

"I never thought he was perfect," Maggie said. "What about your mom?"

Pauline and Liam looked at each other. "We haven't told her yet about, um, us."

From inside, the opening of *Snow White* began to play, and Pauline pulled Liam up to dance. He cooperated, looking self-consciously at Maggie. Then Pauline ducked and pulled Maggie up and twirled her slowly around. Then she pushed Maggie and Liam together.

"Why are you guys so stiff?" she asked, jamming their hands together. "Dance like you know each other. Don't be dorks."

"Pauline."

"Well, are we friends or not?" she asked. "Are we going to fix this or not?"

Liam spun Maggie around once, twice, in his awkward way. But he avoided her eyes. Finally, as soon as Pauline allowed it, Maggie pulled out of his hands and sat back down, feeling like she could disintegrate and be perfectly content with that instead of being here.

Pauline shivered and blew mist rings above her head. "Sorry." She looked sadly down at her mittens. Her voice faltered, then came back. "I had this dream we'd all move somewhere warm together one day. Like Austin. We could go to the Chili Parlor Bar. I could learn guitar and be a singer-songwriter. Liam could build houses. You could work at one of the high-rises, doing something where you wear a suit."

"You have a different life's dream every week," Maggie said. The ice melted, just a crack.

They gazed down on the alley. "We could catch the killer from here. We've got a bird's-eye view," Pauline said.

Suddenly, inside the theater, there was a scream. Pauline's and Maggie's eyes met, and they all three hurried inside to see what had happened.

But it was only the movie. Snow White had bitten the apple, and the witch was cackling.

"I'll be glad when this is all over," Pauline said. "When I can hear a movie witch cackle and not automatically think someone's just been murdered. I have to pee." She looked at both of them thoughtfully, as if second-guessing herself, and then disappeared while the two of them walked back out onto the fire escape.

Maggie and Liam sat down silently on the cold metal.

"Don't you dare say you're sorry," Maggie said, when she

saw him open his mouth.

He closed his lips. Then he started again. But he couldn't help himself.

"I don't think even you can know all the things I'm sorry for," he said. "About the dance and Pauline and being a coward since then. I feel disloyal to Pauline if I come talk to you and disloyal to you no matter what . . ."

His voice crackled a little. He wagged his feet back and forth agitatedly.

"I want to wish it—you know, you and me—never happened. Because then I'd still be your friend, and things would be simple between us. But then I'd wish away all this stuff that was . . ." He searched for words, getting desperate. "That was so . . ." And he didn't have to say it. She could see everything he meant by it—he didn't want to banish the walks in the snow and the times in his room and the sauna. . . . She wondered if life would be easier if people could talk to each other in pictures.

"If this had happened differently." He paused, flustered. "If it hadn't been that I met her so long ago and that she's . . . in my bones. It's been her, ever since I was little. I do love you." Words finally failed him. Which was good, because each word was an arrow in Maggie's heart. She wanted to ask him if he really thought Pauline would stay with him. She changed her mind every five minutes, about everything. But Maggie guessed that was the risk he was willing to take. And she wanted to be above saying such petty things.

Finally she collected herself enough to say something back. "Liam, I think . . . when things happened . . . maybe we were both just missing Pauline." She turned her eyes to his, finally. "It didn't mean . . . so much." She'd never been a good liar, but she thought she was being convincing now. Her voice sounded steady and calm. Liam visibly winced. "We were missing her," Maggie repeated. "We were bored." The words were so small compared to the real feelings. She could have said it had been like being broken open for the first time. But instead she forced her mouth into a thin, steady line.

"You know," she went on, "it's stupid. I'll probably be moving soon. I'll be graduating soon. There's a guy back home. It was all just . . . cabin fever."

Maggie could feel herself hiding; her whole face felt like a mask. She made the wildly hurting parts small inside herself.

Liam had been surprised into silence. His eyes looked wide-open and honest and hurt. But they both knew he had no right to be hurt.

Finally he knotted his hands together in defeat, as if whatever had really needed to be said had been said. "I still don't know why you would have let a crazy person like me get his hands on you."

Maggie softened. All the anger flooded out of her for a moment. "You're not crazy," she said. "It's small towns that are crazy."

"What if people always say that, but really it's never any different? What if everywhere you always felt like that, like somewhere else is the right place and you are in the wrong place? What if it's just a personality trait?"

The door creaked behind them, and Pauline came out on the stairwell. "It's freezing out here," she said, and it sunk in that she was right. They followed her indoors.

On the way home at dawn, Maggie leaned her face against the car window and watched the scenery, pretending to be asleep. When she pulled her face back, the window was wet from where her eyes had been watering, the moisture shot through with the glare of the moonlight bouncing off the snow.

That night Abe barked at the woods until dawn, and no one paid attention to him. Everyone was too wrapped up—completely and passionately—in life. How could anyone who was alive think about being anything else?

Maggie glanced out her window and saw Pauline and Liam lying beside each other in the back field, on an old camping tarp in front of a bonfire. They had zipped two sleeping bags together for warmth. He had her face in his hands and his thumbs lightly on her cheeks. There was the sense that they were the only two—not just alive, but possible and real.

The warmth they created rose like steam from where they lay on the ground and reached and dissipated into the night air. It leaked into the cracks of the houses.

Maggie sat in her bedroom that night, listening to songs

on her dad's old radio. She stared at herself in the mirror—
her scattering of freckles, two tiny beauty marks on her right
cheek, so familiar she could point to them in the dark. Later
she wouldn't understand why she did what she did. She got
out the paints from the back of her closet. She mixed them on
her palette—making lush purples and forest greens and deep
orangey reds out of a tiny bit of cyan, the right amount of yellow, an instinctively well-sized blob of magenta.

She unrolled an old canvas, sat in front of it, and made
one broad, quick stroke of reddish purple. Then she took
the brush and, for no reason she could say, ran it along the
underside of her wrist, leaving a long, thin stripe of the same
color there—like blood, only more deeply dark, more rich.
She painted her elbow and then up along her arm. She turned
to her full-length mirror and painted along the curve of her
neck, and then the insides of her arms. Green, purple, orange.

The smell of campfire smoke wafted in through the min-
iscule spaces around the glass, and the reflection of the moon
on the snow blinked up at her window. Etta sang, and Maggie
painted herself black and blue.

That night a shadow tried to push a girl into a car in downtown Gill Creek, and she managed to scream for help. A
policeman nearby saw the struggle from where he was parked
at the side of the road, got out, and chased the attacker into the
woods. By morning over thirty cops were beating the bushes

and trailing through the trees that stretched back behind Al's Grocery. Though they'd brought dogs in to follow the scent, they'd lost him, his trail vanishing at the lake's edge, as if he'd walked across the ice to the middle of nowhere.

23

MAGGIE AWOKE TO PAULINE'S VOICE IN THE YARD, CALLING FOR ABE. HER MOM was in the kitchen looking over a finance book, studying for her second interview with the bank in Chicago.

When Maggie walked outside, pulling her coat and boots on over her pajamas, Pauline was standing in the middle of the field at the clothesline, staring out at the woods and huddling in her long, thin, plaid coat. A light breeze blew tiny ice crystals against their faces.

"I haven't seen him for two days," Pauline said. "I thought he'd at least be back when I woke up this morning. He spent another whole night out somewhere. You think he's okay?"

Maggie nodded. "Yeah. Of course." She tried to sound

confident to reassure Pauline. But it wasn't like Abe to let her out of his sight.

"Do you think someone took him?"

"No." Maggie shook her head. "No, that's crazy. He's probably off looking for some girl dogs. He'll be back."

"My mom called the ASPCA," Pauline said. "I can tell she doesn't think he's coming back. She adores that dog—you wouldn't think so, because she never pets him—but she does. He lost one of his tags." Pauline held up a little red tag, then dropped it again in the snow.

She looked out at the back lot, where Abe had stood guard between the house and the woods. "He watches out for me," she said plaintively. "I just know something's happened to him." Pauline stared into the trees. "We're meeting Aunt Cylla halfway for breakfast," she said, tossing back her head in frustration. "She and Mom are doing a benefit together this weekend in Milwaukee, courtesy of Tidings Tea. Mom says I have to go."

"Do you wanna come inside for a few minutes?"

Pauline followed Maggie in and up to her room. She pulled off her scarf but kept her coat on, trying to warm up. Maggie turned on the radio while Pauline ran her fingers along Maggie's books.

"I wish I had your brain," Pauline said. "I have no attention span."

Her fingers lit on Maggie's sketchbook, and Maggie moved forward to pull it away from her, but it was too late. Pauline had opened to a random page and stared down at the picture Maggie had drawn. It was of Pauline, her hair falling over her shoulder in a soft braid, some wisps wild and escaped, her eyes faraway, lit up but also a little sad. Maggie had drawn it from memory. She'd done another perspective on the next page, from behind, and had included Pauline's scar down the side of her back—like a stripe on a beautiful flower—as if she would have been missing something without it.

Pauline looked up at her, eyes wide.

"I don't see myself like this," Pauline said.

"See yourself how?"

Pauline touched her finger to the drawn face. "You make it look like I have a beautiful soul."

Pauline flipped through the pages. Through drawings of Abe and Maggie's mom and the house, her dad poised over a banister sanding it, the sauna in the woods. "I thought you gave it up, drawing."

"I picked it up again recently."

Pauline settled on a flower Maggie had drawn. It was a winter flower, delicate, vivid. "That's like you."

Maggie smirked and rolled her eyes. "That's a flower."

"Yeah." Pauline pulled back the book. She went on flipping the pages. And just as Maggie remembered that the back pages were full of Liam, Pauline came to them. There were Liam's hands; there was the model ship hanging from Liam's window. Maggie hadn't drawn Liam himself. It had felt overwhelming to look at him that long.

Pauline put down the sketchbook and thought for a long time. She went to the window, crossed her thin arms, and sighed. "It's hard to look at that stuff. I get jealous. But I'm grateful." She nibbled at her dry lips, thinking, working something out. "I don't think it would have ever happened if there was no you and Liam. When I saw you two together, that night at the Turkey Gobble, before we went and set off the fireworks . . . that's when I first thought . . ."

Maggie tried to take it in. Pauline had seen what was happening between them, and it had made her *jealous*?

"You never tried to just be happy for me?" she asked, her stomach churning.

Pauline turned to her. "Maggie, I've known Liam since I can remember. It's not just . . . some fling."

Fling? Pauline was starting to look flustered, like she knew she was saying all the wrong things. "It's hot in here," she said agitatedly. She unbuttoned her coat and pulled it off. And there was . . . it.

Maggie just stared. She was wearing it. The dress. Seafoam green. Tiny airplanes.

"You got that dress?" Maggie blurted out.

Pauline seemed to remember the dress and shrugged. "From my mom." She looked perfect in it. "Oh, I have this for you," Pauline said suddenly. She picked up her coat, reached into the pocket, and put something into Maggie's hands. It was the bracelet Maggie had sent her in the mail. "I get why you gave it to me. Because Liam gave it to you. But we want you to have it. *I* want you to have it."

Maggie cupped the bracelet in her hand. She moved her palm so that the cherry charm dangled back and forth. It should have come with a charm that said, *I took a chance and all I got was this lousy bracelet.* But she still couldn't get over the dress. She wondered, with building rage, if Pauline would get everything she wanted her whole life—Liam, the dress, jobs, whatever—because she was beautiful and rich. She wondered, maliciously, if Liam would even *love* Pauline if it weren't for her looks. If Pauline were ugly, would Liam have left Maggie? She clung tightly and bitterly to the thought.

"He cares about you," Pauline said, as if it weren't possible for the words to hurt. Maggie didn't reply; she kept her rage inside like a weapon. Sensing she'd worn out her welcome, Pauline went home a few minutes later, pulling her heavy coat back on again and stomping off with bare legs across the field.

The living always think that monsters roar and gnash their teeth. But I've seen that real monsters can be friendly; they can smile, and they can say please and thank you like everyone else. Real monsters can appear to be kind. Sometimes they can be inside us.

I can't quite stay in this moment. I'm peeling away from it. Something bothers me—and it isn't just that the hole in the cellar is wider than ever, big enough for me. I can't concentrate. There's something about this time, an answer gnawing at me, and after a few moments it takes shape. And it fills me with a terrified heat.

I think I know. Why these people, why this place, why now, why me.

24

THE ADULTS OF WATER STREET HAD ALREADY MADE THEIR PLANS BY THE time the forecast came. The weather that would arrive after they'd gone was sweeping the whole Midwest. All over the middle top of the country sleepy towns and cities were muffled under snow and temperatures that made their bones rattle. In Minnesota and North Dakota, animals froze in their pens.

"You'll just have to come with us. I don't want to leave you alone." Mrs. Larsen stood at the foot of her bed, laying a pair of pumps into her suitcase. Maggie sat propped up against the headboard, watching.

"Mom, please. I'll be fine. I have a ton of schoolwork right now. And Pauline's mom will be here." She remembered after she'd spoken that, actually, Pauline's mom would be in Milwaukee. But by then her mom was looking halfway soothed.

"Mom, this is our *house*; we have to feel safe here. I'm not going to go anywhere. I'll just stay in with the alarm on till you get back. I'll keep the doors locked and everything. Really, it's not a big deal. I'll stay in."

Her mom studied her. "Maybe you could have Pauline and her mom stay over."

"Sure, I'll ask her," Maggie lied. She didn't want to ask Pauline. But she knew her mom was being overly cautious.

Her parents packed the last of their things, and Maggie helped her mom lug her suitcase down the stairs. They ate a quick dinner together, and then Maggie got up and did the dishes while her mom gathered up her purse and coat. They bundled themselves up and surveyed the room, as if trying to think of anything they'd forgotten.

"Are you sure, honey?" her dad asked.

"Definitely," Maggie said.

"Call me if you need anything," her mom said.

Maggie nodded impatiently as she locked the door behind them.

She watched a couple of shows and then some cable news for a while. Everyone was talking about the approaching storm, and around ten her mom called to check on her and make her go over where the flashlights and the generator were. Pauline called around ten thirty and asked if she wanted to meet at the sauna tomorrow around five. Liam's dad was going to be out late at a job, and Liam had a bunch of chores to do, so they could go naked and not worry about him happening by. Maggie agreed, although she didn't really feel like seeing Pauline. She climbed the stairs and crawled in bed with a book.

The house should have felt big and warm around her with the weather picking up outside—she usually loved that feeling. But tonight, with her parents gone, her ears perked up at every little sound outside: the crunching of branches, the gusts rattling the old doors as they sent drafts through the house. The house itself creaked so much in the wind that it sounded like someone was walking along the floors. She drifted off to sleep while the wind blew the weather in—it buffeted the windows and made the covers feel cozier. It seemed, in her half-dream state, as if all of Water Street—all the world—was empty, white, silent, waiting.

By the next morning, the storm had taken down the phone lines three streets away. Maggie discovered there was no connection when she went to call Pauline and make up an excuse about not meeting her at the sauna. She looked out the window and considered walking over to tell her in person but decided against it. She'd figure it out when Maggie didn't show. She knew her mom would be worried and thought maybe she should go wander around to try to find a signal to text her. But when she stepped out onto the deck, it was so frigid and windy that she ducked back inside to wait for everything to calm down.

The wind has died and left a waiting silence—the kind of quiet that promises the bigger storm to come. I float above the peninsula and wonder: How do you lose the thread of your own story, the one you are supposed to know by heart?

Because, looking down on the snow-tipped trees, I know now I've seen this story before. It feels like it makes up the shape of my heart . . . or the ball of moths where my heart should be.

I watch Pauline waiting under a stand of pine trees at dusk, looking in the direction of Maggie's house. She's brought binoculars for bird-watching. Her breath rises in puffs, and she shivers in her thin, seventies-style plaid coat; she tugs tighter on her off-white, knit hat. Underdressed as usual, she hasn't worn leggings or pants; her bare legs peek out from under her coat.

Not a soul has emerged from Maggie's house, aside from me. But Pauline isn't alone.

He's standing at the edge of the woods. He must have hiked in from the snow-plowed main road, because the snow's piled too high for cars here.

James Falk only watches Pauline quietly from the road for a moment, then turns back in the direction he's come, as if sneaking away from her. Instead of following his tracks all the way back down Water Street, he turns in the direction of Liam Witte's house, cutting across the field. I realize she's not the one he's come for, and I follow him.

Liam's taken advantage of the lull in the weather to come outside and grab some dry wood from the shed, which is far across the field from his house. He's just crossing the clearing back toward his house when he looks up to see the figure at the edge of the field. He stands and wipes his hands on his pants and starts walking toward him, recognizing him. There's a moment when he still seems to think everything is okay. He only seems puzzled as James stands there without saying anything, looking at him like he might bolt. But it's only a moment before he clearly feels the fear. He keeps his hands in his pockets and smiles at James. He lifts his left hand to wave.

James coils, and Liam pauses midstep. And then James is hurtling. Liam backs up, stumbling, and as he reaches him, holds his hands in front of his face reflexively. Still, he isn't prepared for the fist as it rips across his nose.

He pivots and pulls away quickly, leaving a

growing white swath of ground between them, blood flying off the side of his face. But he's chosen the wrong direction, toward the fence that lines this part of Water Street.

He comes up hard against it, and James slams up behind him as he tries to climb. He's halfway over before James pulls him down. Fists fly, but they only belong to James—Liam's hands are only palms, trying to stop and deflect.

At some point the snow starts again, softly but persistently, falling into the tracks they've both left across the snow and onto James's shoulders as he pounds and pounds. And then Liam's head hits the fence with a shudder. Liam goes limp. James pulls back, scared now, because of the blood staining the snow beside Liam's head.

He backs up, then turns and runs.

I want to help. I want to shine a giant spotlight on the boy lying in the snow and on the one running for his car.

But I'm only the ghost, a memory of a memory.

These moments are all in the past. What can anyone do about them now?

25

I retreat to a quiet moment, back before this night. Just a regular night weeks before, when nothing is happening. I sit at the window of Maggie's room.

A spider makes a web in the white glow of the floodlights. I watch her work; the moths flutter in her web. Some of them are too big for her to eat or are not to her taste. They're just in the wrong place at the wrong time.

But not me. There's nothing accidental about me being in this place, and this time. I've sifted through these hours—I've hovered above Water Street and below it in dark spaces—because of what I've done and what I need to atone for.

I'm afraid I know what it is, and I don't want to know.

The moonlight on this night, weeks before, is beautiful. The people I love are still living. There's so much peace here. I want to stay forever. But time pulls me forward.

A key is buried in the dirt under the front stairs of the house on Water Street. The word Subaru is etched across its face in faded letters.

If I still breathed air, I'd take a breath.

＊ ＊ ＊

Pauline walks along the snowy road in her black winter boots, trudging in the direction of the Wittes' and gazing up at the cardinal that seems to be following her from tree to tree. It's been snowing for about an hour, but only lightly, and every few moments pieces of the sunset shine through the clouds and filter down through the trees.

She walks up to the house and knocks and waits. She peers across the empty field and sees the dim outline of Liam's tracks, strangely crisscrossed and jumbled. She knocks again.

Pauline stamps her feet together and rubs her mittens against each other, then turns and walks back to the edge of Water Street. She must be thinking that he's gone on a walk or that he's gone to her house, straight through the woods, and they've passed each other. She peers into the trees in the hopes of seeing Abe.

She sighs. She starts off again in the direction of home.

As she walks back down Water Street, she glances at the field beyond the fence, staring again at the crisscrossed tracks. She listens to the silence and glances at the silo in the distance. Then keeps walking. She's almost at the edge of the fence when she stops and backtracks a few steps, staring at something. Under the shelter of an evergreen that overhangs the fence, where there's only a light dusting of snow because of the full branches, there are drops of dark red. Blood.

At first she thinks it must be an animal. Pauline looks to either side of her and then sees the tracks. Whatever it is has set a definite course. The trail—the deep furrow in the snow—leads toward the silo.

She walks through a scattering of evergreens, and now the path opens up into the wider clearing, and from here, the trail leads right to the silo door, which has been left open.

Pauline's eyes water with fear; she wipes them with her mittens. Not an animal.

She walks forward slowly now, tense. She pauses at the threshold and peers into the shadowy darkness inside the silo.

She only has to push the door a little farther—letting the last of the evening light in—to see the figure. It's curled on top of a pile of grain.

It stirs and rattles. Its breath is labored.

The figure has a voice. It calls her by her name.

Maggie stood in front of the full-length mirror in her bedroom, trying on her blue-flowered dress. It fell to just above her knees, and she liked the way it clung to her hips and accentuated her curves. But there was no denying it was still an ugly dress.

She thought of her dad walking into the store to buy it and kept trying to look at it from a different angle, hoping to magically change her mind.

She wondered if her mom had realized, as soon as she'd seen the dress, that it was all wrong. She was just starting to unzip it when a choked, metallic groan pulled her attention to the window. She could see Pauline's silhouette in the front seat of the old Subaru across the yard, trying to get it started. Maggie wondered absently where she was trying to go in the crazy weather. The car had snow tires, but that didn't mean it could plow its way through a foot of snow. She turned to her dresser and rezipped her dress. Maybe if she sat with it a while longer, it would grow on her.

A few moments later, out of the corner of her eye, she noticed Pauline's dark shape crossing the snowy field between their houses at a faltering run, like she was tripping through the snow. Maggie leaned her face up against the window in curiosity as Pauline raced up onto the porch.

She heard the doorbell ring below and then the pounding on the door, the loud staccato of Pauline's fist.

Maggie turned toward the hall, then hesitated. There was something Pauline *urgently* wanted to tell her. Or something she wanted to do immediately and couldn't wait for. Whatever it was, it was another thing that would end up revolving around Pauline. Maggie's heart pounded in her chest with envy and anger. If she'd had boiling oil right then, like they'd had on the walls of castles in the Middle Ages, she might have poured it out her window.

She turned back toward her mirror. She smoothed out the skirt of the dress with her hands. She decided that, no matter how hard Pauline knocked, she wouldn't answer the door.

26

Pauline Boden is shaking so hard, her hands jerk like puppets. She clutches the Subaru key in her hand.

Panting and trembling on the Larsen porch, she pounds on the door, then steps back and looks up at Maggie's window, which is bright while the rest of the house is dark.

"Maggie!" she yells. But her voice comes out raspy and useless. She turns back to the door and pounds harder. She stares up at Maggie's window as if willing her out, but the kitchen stays dark; nobody comes. She runs a circle around the house, trying all the doors, pulling at the windows, and then comes back up the stairs to the front door and pounds on it again.

Her lips, her whole face shaking, she is becoming defeated. She's gone from disbelieving to desperate to slack.

She nods to herself, muttering. She'll try the car again. She remembers her dad once drove through worse, when she was sick with appendicitis.

She pivots on the stoop and takes two jarring steps down. The moment the key slips through her numb fingers, Pauline lets out a strangled gasp. She watches it slide between the slats in the deck and fall underneath. "No," she whispers.

She leaps down over the next two steps and falls to her knees, patting the ground around the steps. She tries to reach underneath, but the underside is blocked by wooden supports. "No no no," she says, her voice like the high whine of a car. "No." She tries to reach her hands under, kicks the wood, digs at the snow. It's useless. The key is gone.

Silent tears spill onto her cheeks.

And then she turns and looks toward the lake.

27

MAGGIE WAS READING THE LAST PAGES OF *ANNA KARENINA* AND WATCHING the snow outside her window whip itself up into a blizzard. The temperature on the thermometer had dropped since the last time she'd looked at it in the kitchen window, though it had already been frigid to start with.

Something kept making her get up and look out the window toward Pauline's house.

Finally, after looking over for what seemed like the millionth time, she gave up on her book. She stood and walked downstairs, pulled her heavy coat on over her dress, and yanked her heavy snow boots over her socks. Her legs were bare, but it was only a short walk to Pauline's porch.

Once outside her front door, she noticed the snow-muted dips of Pauline's tracks—one set leading up and another back down the stairs, and a confused bunching of prints at the bottom. The tracks coming to her house led to the car that Pauline had been trying to start, but the others led away. Maggie stared at them for a moment in confusion, tasting the iciness in the air.

The cold gnawed at her knees and her hands . . . at every bit of her that she'd left uncovered. She followed the tracks through the dark, barely making them out with so little moonlight through the cloud- and snow-obscured sky. Worry made her pulse speed up. The tracks inexplicably continued out across the field and—Maggie stood shocked and disbelieving—onto the ice. A lump in her throat, she looked back toward her house, then again in the direction of the tracks disappearing across the lake . . . toward the glittering, far-away lights of Gill Creek.

Her heart was pounding now, and she felt a little sick. Something had happened. Something was very wrong. Pauline had gone out on the ice. She was walking in the direction of Gill Creek. *Pauline had gone out on the ice.*

Maggie felt like she had moments to decide what to do. She walked to the edge of the snow-covered beach.

She put a foot out onto the snowy, gritty, slippery surface. And then another, testing. She picked up speed with each step.

* * *

It could have been five minutes or fifteen. Maggie only knew that she'd made up her mind to trust that the lake was truly frozen through, because she was deep into it now, and the tracks went farther, even as they were disappearing under the driving snow.

At first she wasn't sure whether the dark speck ahead was a person. As she got closer, there was no doubt—Pauline's skinny frame was silhouetted against the snowflakes, moving away from her, barely there at all.

"Pauline!" she screamed.

The figure came to a halt and seemed to swivel. An arm rose to wave as its owner shifted to the left.

And then she disappeared. *Whoosh.*

Maggie didn't scream or think. Her mind went as clean and clear as an animal's; she wasn't even afraid. She just knew that she had to get to Pauline. She sprinted, trying to keep her bearings toward where Pauline had been a moment before. She slid along the ice, to where it had splintered into a gaping gash in the snow, and threw herself flat. She plunged her arms into the icy water.

For a moment she felt nothing, only the searing pain of the frigid water digging right into her bones. Then she felt hair like cobwebs around her right hand, and she grabbed a fistful, then groped for Pauline's shoulder, the long line of her arm. She tried to pull her out, but the ice crumbled at the edges. She shimmied backward, holding on to Pauline's wrist, and tried again. Pauline's head had surfaced now; she was sputtering and grasping Maggie's hands loosely, as if her fingers couldn't close into a real grip.

Finally Maggie forced herself still for a moment, agonizing as it was. She thought about where she was, distributed her weight better, and got a better hold of Pauline, under one arm. She scooted herself forward for leverage, but not too far forward. She leveraged her up slightly and then pulled. Once Pauline's chest was on the ice, Maggie scooted back, slowly again. Pauline was mostly still. Maggie tugged her back, farther out of the water, inch by inch.

Pauline lay on the ice, shivering and jerking. Maggie pulled off her coat and wrapped it around her, so that now she was wearing only the ugly dress and boots.

After a few moments, she stood and hoisted Pauline upward and against her as much as she could.

"You gotta walk, Pauline. I'm not strong enough to carry you." Pauline moved forward like spaghetti. "He's hurt," she said tiredly. "We have to get someone to come."

"Who's hurt?" Maggie asked. But she knew the only person she could mean.

Maggie looked in the direction of downtown Gill Creek, then back in the direction of home. She longed to turn back toward her house with every inch of her body. But by now, she reasoned, they were as far into the lake as they were out. It wasn't for sure that one was closer than the other, because she couldn't see home. But at least she could see town, small and far-off as it seemed, and she turned their steps in that direction.

They walked for about fifteen minutes without saying a word, just focusing on putting their feet forward. Pauline was slow at first but then seemed to gather strength as they walked, even though she shivered violently and the snow seemed to fall harder as the minutes dragged on. It took Maggie several minutes to realize that she too was wet through, from the top of her dress down. The top of her head felt numb and frozen without a hat. She'd never imagined cold like what she felt. It was stabbing pain all over her scalp and shoulders. She envied Pauline the coat she'd given her, but she didn't take it back; she just wrapped her left arm tighter around her. Her terror of falling through the ice at any minute shrank into the background just slightly behind the icy pain of freezing, inch by inch.

The lights seemed to get only marginally bigger as they walked. Maggie began to wonder if really they'd been as close as she'd thought. And then Pauline interrupted her thoughts.

"So, do you come here often?" She smiled, looking near-delirious.

Maggie opened her mouth to speak and sucked in a lung-ful of cold air. "I'm practicing for the Olympics too. The 'cross-country frigid death march.'"

"I think anything less than the silver dies a frozen death," Pauline said, her voice underlined by fear.

By now the air seemed to be more snow than oxygen, and

the wind was working hard against them. Maggie remembered the wind tunnels the streets made back in Chicago, how they seemed to spit the wind right through your skin into your organs. That had been nothing compared to the wind whipping at them now across the open lake.

Pauline was slowing down, and Maggie could feel her legs turning into jelly—frozen jelly but jelly nonetheless.

"Jell-O pops," she said out loud.

"What?" Pauline asked.

"Nothing," Maggie muttered. She felt loopy. Her scalp wasn't in quite so much pain though. "We should have turned back," she said, but Pauline either didn't hear her or just didn't have the strength to answer. "We're stupid," Maggie added anyway. "We're fatally stupid."

There was a shape up ahead. It was impossible that there could be, because they were still way out on the lake, but there it was, nonetheless. Pauline saw it too; she lifted her arm and pointed.

It grew and grew, so she knew they were getting closer.

Finally she made out what it was. It was the hull of an old, rusted ship, sticking up out of the water. It was the eeriest sight she'd ever seen, and it also seemed impossible. But Pauline was pulling her toward it with her babylike lack of strength, and Maggie let herself be pulled.

They walked right up behind the hull; it was maybe only ten feet above the surface, but behind it the air suddenly went blessedly quiet, relatively speaking.

"Do you think the ice somehow pushed it up?" Maggie asked. "Like, made the air bring it up?"

"It blocks the wind," Pauline said, then shook up and down the length of her body.

They huddled against the decayed metal, pushing up against it as tightly as they could and put their arms around each other. Pauline was still shivering like crazy. But the longer they sat, the less she shivered. Maggie glanced toward the lights of Gill Creek, so tempting, seemingly so close, and then she ducked back her head, thinking they'd wait a little while longer behind the welcome windbreak. Pauline was as pale as the snow; her eyes looked like big, black bruises in the eerie half-light of the moon trying to peek through the clouds.

"You came to get me," she said finally, as if she were just realizing it.

Maggie nodded.

"You're my great friend," Pauline said. "And I'm sorry. I'm so, so sorry."

"You're mine too," Maggie said. "And I'm going to forgive you. When I can."

Pauline looked around, as if in disbelief at where they'd found themselves. She seemed to come back to herself more every minute. "Maggie," she finally said, now sounding completely alert. "Do you think we could die here?"

"No." Maggie shook her head, her whole body feeling numb. She felt punchy, almost giddy. "That doesn't happen.

That's the kind of thing that happens in, like, 1832. To, like, explorers."

"I know, but I'm so cold," Pauline said, coughing a ragged laugh.

"I won't let it happen. I'll look out for you." Maggie blew on her hands. She talked to keep herself feeling like herself. "You know, we have so much to do. We can't die."

Pauline huddled closer to her. Maggie felt numb; the thin fabric of her dress was about as useful as being naked. She couldn't think right.

She tried to get warm by thinking about her parents in some warm hotel in Chicago or about being on the beach in Florida. She thought about drinking tropical drinks and sleeping under a palm-frond fan. Maggie wanted to sleep under a palm tree sometime. She promised herself she would.

"Maggie?" Pauline shifted.

"Yeah?"

"Just making sure."

"It's gonna be okay," Maggie heard her own voice say. She wanted to tell Pauline she was sorry about her envy, the dark pieces of her heart that were hard and jealous, but it seemed less important than the warmth; it seemed small and silly and forgettable. "We'll get somewhere warm," she said, "as soon as the snow lets up."

She seemed to be there already.

28

PAULINE WOKE WITH A JERK, BLINKING IN THE BRIGHT SUN.

Light was beaming down from a blue sky, as if the snow-storm had never happened at all.

She pulled her coat around her and stood up fast, spots swimming in front of her eyes with the sudden movement. It took only a moment to come back to her. Liam, Maggie, getting to town. She peered around the side of the hull, her heart picking up speed.

They were closer to the edge of the lake than she'd thought last night. In the distance gray clouds were just drifting off over Lake Michigan, dissipating, moving away from one another at top speed. The sun was picking its way out and up from the horizon, warm-looking and orangey yellow, a pure morning sun that cast its early, bright rays on Pauline's face.

She stared out across the ice, dazed, frigid. Then she turned her sights back along the rocky shore of the lake and toward town and then pivoted and hurried back toward Maggie.

She knelt beside her to wake her and was bewildered, at first, when she didn't respond. She put a hand on Maggie's thin sleeve, remembering that she'd slept in Maggie's coat, that Maggie had wrapped it around her. Her confusion suddenly collapsed into concern and then panic as she took both of Maggie's arms.

"Maggie," she said. "Maggie, wake up." She sank back on her heels, wiped fast tears from her cheeks, and said it again. "Mags. We have to go."

Just around the hull, a shaft of light rose high enough to fall onto Maggie's face, but she couldn't see it—not with living eyes.

Still, I saw it anyway. I saw it all.

29

I've read articles; I've seen it in magazines: It's dangerous to be young. When I was alive, I watched scary movies where young, beautiful girls were the first to die. I read magazines that told me all about how young actresses fell from great heights—how they got cellulite or turned into sloppy drunks or got into car accidents that were their fault. I once read about a girl who was kidnapped from the Walmart parking lot because her attacker liked the color of her hair. I suppose beauty can be dangerous too.

Pauline's physical beauty was the smallest part of

her. It distracted some people from seeing her. Sometimes, even me.

I know now I'm not here to take care of unfinished business or to get revenge or to set right something I did wrong, like you read about in ghost stories. I did right. And that's left me knowing this: I'm still here, simply because it's hard to leave. I'm here trying to say goodbye. I'm watching my life and my world flash before my eyes, but slowly, because that's the right way for a person to make an exit.

It was always my story I was trying to learn.

I venture out of Door County. I float over the flat heat of Texas, down across the low, brown hills to Austin, moths trailing in my wake. (If it's possible, there are more of them than ever.) I spot her from light-years away; her messy hair, her jerky movements, her way of trying to hide her looks.

I don't know what year it is, but I can see she's in her early twenties. She must be on her lunch break, because she's stuffing a chili dog into her mouth as if it's her last meal on earth, but I know it won't be. I know she has a long and happy life ahead of her. I know that, inside the bar, she plays songs for tips and sings like a bird.

But when she gets a break, she comes out to sit on the curb and soak up her beloved heat. Abe sits beside her, gray around the jowls, and gets the last bite. I don't know how they found each other again, after I died; I haven't seen that moment yet and I guess I never will. I do know Pauline only plays at bars that allow her to bring him with her.

She sits there on the curb with her face to the sun, moving on to her fries. Inside, a song is playing on the jukebox, and she listens all the way through, drinks the last of a Coke, and smooths out her tight, sparkly jeans and her tank top, then scratches Abe's ears. She never seems to sense that I am there. She twirls her wedding ring around her finger when she sees him.

He walks up the street in a white T-shirt stained with grease. He's been working on cars, but he always times his lunch breaks around hers. He's filled out since his teens; his arms are thicker, his body is more muscular, and his face is older—but his skin is still that boarding-school creamy pale.

He sits beside her without a word, and they fight over her fries with their fingers. I know they talk about me; I know they try to keep me alive and with them all the time. But today they say nothing.

I don't know if there's a heaven or not, but I like to imagine anyway that the angels made me and that they did it carefully. They kneaded my skin into arms and legs. They caressed my human shape and patted it down so that everything would look right. They gave me a few extra caresses too, because they knew they were sending me into life on earth, and they knew life on earth can break your heart. They gave me a brain for a helmet. They massaged a heart in through the backs of my ribs so that I could feel pain and know when to back up. I haven't seen the angels yet, but I wouldn't be surprised if they appear. Like I said, there are so many things I was wrong about.

For instance, I used to think that things, in the end—if it was really the end—turned out neat, clean, and symmetrical. But that's not how it is. And I know this because I know that the Door County Killer was never caught, that he was a stranger to us, and that we were just unlucky when he came onto the peninsula that fall. It could have been anywhere. He never killed again in our county after that winter. I don't know why—what brain chemicals set him loose and what reined him in.

I've seen the moment of his death, on a ferry in

southwest Canada, in his later years—unfairly, too late. The ferry sinks, and he's stuck in the bathroom—just the wrong place at the wrong time. Like Hairica, and those other girls. I guess maybe that's symmetrical after all.

You can see his skeleton if you want; you just have to sink down into the river. If I had hands and time, I'd scatter his bones and wait for them to dissolve for millions of years if I had to.

But it's nearing time for me to dissolve, myself.

I've already said good-bye to my parents; I've drifted through their new apartment in Chicago more than once. I know what they've lost and what they've gained: I've seen the nights when they're awake until morning from grief. I've seen the days when they've started to feel slightly alive again, scattered among so many steps backward. I've watched them pack and sell the house, get new jobs, and leave Door County the same way they came in. I've watched my mom standing in the kitchen holding a toddler just to feel him close to her. They're not blood, but they're connected. He has big, brown eyes and hyper legs, and he's the most beautiful thing. I wish I could teach him what I know, but I guess that's a pretty common wish for those who've already lived. I

wish that I could be his guardian angel. But I know I'm
not allowed to stay.

   I turn away from Austin. I drift up over Wisconsin,
along Washington Island, over birds, the ocean, Canada, Alaska, the North Pole. A pleasure trip around the
beautiful northern world. And then I turn south again.
There's one more thing I know I'll see, a last piece of the
past that's waiting to take me with itself.

*It's January, and Liam and I are in the car driving
north; he's taking me on the surprise that's just for me.
I'm eating a bag of chips while Liam tries to navigate.
It's quiet as we pull into a deserted parking lot surrounded by tall trees. We get out, and Liam leads me
along a dim, wooded trail. And suddenly the trees open
out, and there before us is the most beautiful spring,
crystal-blue-white and practically glowing. We strip
down to our underwear in the cold air and, though I'm
scared because I can't swim, I trust him. He holds my
hand as we slide into the water, and we suck in our
breath from the change in temperature; the water feels
warm against the frigid air. I float my arms around his
neck and wrap my legs around his waist, holding on to
his back.*

He tows me into the middle of the spring, and we can see the trout swimming underneath us, circling flecks of silver. Liam laughs, and it echoes around the spring, but no one is there to hear but me—the ghost me and the living me.

Beneath us the water dances, and the sand far, far below bubbles like clouds. We're floating over heaven. It's our perfect moment, and it never disappears. Even now I can see us, even long after the moment is gone. Love can't be taken back once it's given.

Liam says, "I've got you." And moves me from his back, holding one hand against my stomach. I know what he wants.

I stretch out my arms, like I've seen other people do, and I push my legs behind me, and—with his hand there to catch me—I swim.

This is what I think the world is showing me. We are souls at a common cause. We are only here to love. That was my great story all along. We are here to take chances, and fail, and keep trying.

I'm back in the cellar on Water Street, alone, and the hole is big enough for me. I can't seem to stop moving toward the brightness. The curiosity is overwhelming me now.

If only I could take even one thing with me. Just a bracelet or a slip of paper or even the memory of a duckling or even a sound or a line from a song. Just one memory to remind me of who I am would make all the difference.

I want to have a last look at something real. I catch glimpses of other times and other moments, but they go quickly. A woman stands in the empty field above, before the house is built. The field is buzzing with grasshoppers, and as the woman walks, butterflies and moths spring out of the tall grass around her feet. The view, the clean breeze, it seems like a place where only happy things could ever happen. "We'll build it right here," she says to the man walking behind her. As if she can picture the house exactly as it should be—a wide porch, where she can sit and catch the lake breezes, a sweeping yard, dormers for the upstairs windows; the perfect place to begin a life. She spins the cherry bracelet on her wrist. She touches her stomach, where life is growing. The future is everything to her.

And then I'm past it.

Suddenly I fear what's coming next. I try to remember all my favorite songs. I run through as many as I can.

I step inside the bright hole, of my own free will, and here I see the last thing I was expecting to find. It's my grave. There's my headstone, and underneath the dirt I see my bones.

But I'm not in them. I have nothing to do with my bones at all. I'm something else. I realize that I'm bigger than my bones and bigger than my cellar and bigger than Door County. I'm part of something that's made entirely of me, and yet of which I'm only a speck, a small piece. It turns out I'm not alone.

Suddenly I'm smiling. I feel as big and wide as the earth or the universe or even bigger, like I will disappear, but I will never really disappear. It turns out death is something of a joke. It's indescribably funny. And I laugh. The world seems to open up—crack open—sing.

There's a feeling of lightness in the air. And this is when the moths disperse. They fly apart, a flurry of night colors: dusk green and twilight blue and luminous white. They circle out; they're like the eye of a hurricane, and they're rising. Their beauty makes me want to cry, but then I realize it's my beauty, I'm them and they're me, and I'm flying apart too, going in a thousand different directions, each of which will end only God knows where. We, the moths and me, are like tiny angels ourselves. We circle toward a million moons, a million points of lights. And then, as if my life were a tiny pinprick of light in a long, beautiful, mysterious night, I go. I am gone.

ACKNOWLEDGMENTS

THANK YOU TO SARAH LANDIS FOR HER KEEN INSIGHTS AND EFFORTS, Rosemary Stimola for always giving me such a firm foundation and sounding board, and Melinda Weigel for her work behind the scenes. Thanks to Tasha Diakides for the early brainstorming sessions and Crunchie bars, Katie Pavia for introducing me to the Neko Case song "Margaret vs. Pauline," and Carrie Chimenti and the Wigleys for enticing me to Door County. Thanks always to Mark, my most beloved and handsome critique partner, and to my family.

I've taken many liberties with Door County, a beautiful place that to my knowledge contains no killers. The Door County I've written about is partly imaginary—I've created towns, schools, people, churches, and a villain that doesn't exist. But I do want to point out that the real Door County is pretty wonderful.

Read on for more from
JODI LYNN ANDERSON

She stands on the cliffs, near the old crumbling stone house.

There's nothing left in the house but an upturned table, a ladle, and a clay bowl. She stands for more than an hour, goose-bumped and shivering. At these times, she won't confide in me. She runs her hands over her body, as if checking that it's still there, her heart pulsing and beating. The limbs are smooth and strong, thin and sinewy, her hair long and black and messy and gleaming despite her age. You wouldn't know it to look at her, that she's lived long enough to look for what's across the water. Eighty years later, and she is still fifteen.

These days, there is no new world. The maps have long since settled and stayed put. People know the shapes of Africa, Asia, and South America. And they know which beasts were mythical and which weren't. Manatees are real, mermaids aren't.

Rhinoceroses exist and sea monsters don't. There are no more sea serpents guarding deadly whirlpools. There are pirates, yes, but there is nothing romantic about them. The rest is all stories, and stories have been put in their place.

Now, the outsiders keep their eyes on their own shores, and we keep our eyes on ours. Too far off route, we've been overlooked, and most of us don't think about the world outside. Only she and I are different. Every month or so she comes here and stares toward the ocean, and all the village children whisper about her, even her own. It has become such a ritual.

And when she surfaces from her dream, she calls me by my old name, though no one uses it anymore. And she turns to me, her eyelashes fluttering in the glare that surrounds me, and whispers to me in one short syllable.

Tink.

ONE

L et me tell you something straight off. This is a love
story, but not like any you've heard. The boy and
the girl are far from innocent. Dear lives are lost.
And good doesn't win. In some places, there is something
ultimately good about endings. In Neverland, that is not the
case.

To understand what it's like to be a faerie, tall as a walnut
and genetically gifted with wings—who happened to witness
such a series of events—you must first understand that
all faeries are mute. Somewhere in our evolution, on our
long crooked journey from amoeba to dragonfly to faerie,
nature must have decided language wasn't necessary for us
to survive. It's good in some ways, not to have a language.
It makes you *see* things. You turn your attention, not to

babbling about yourself, broadcasting each and every thought to everyone within earshot—as people often do—but to observing. That's how faeries became so empathic. We're so attuned to the beating of a heart, the varied thrum of a pulse, the zaps of the synapses of a brain, that we are almost inside others' minds. Most faeries tune this out by only spending time with other faeries. They make settlements in tree stumps and barely venture out except to hunt mosquitoes. I get bored by that. I like to fly and keep an eye on things. That was how I saw it, from the beginning. Some would like to call it being nosy. That's what my mother would say, at least.

That morning, I was on my way to see about some locusts. They'd invaded and eaten all the good parts of a faerie settlement near the river, and I had never seen a locust before. I was flying along on a curiosity mission when I passed the girls in a manioc field.

They were out cultivating the tubers—in the tribe, a woman's job. All in their early teens: some of the girls were awkwardly growing but still thoroughly in their skin, with gangly limbs that expressed their most passing thoughts, while others were curvy, and carrying those curves like new tools they were learning. I recognized Tiger Lily instantly; I had seen her before. She stood out like a combination of a roving panther and a girl. She *stalked* instead of walked. Her body still held the invincibility of a child, when at her age it should have been giving way to fragile, flexible curves.

These were Sky Eaters, a tribe whose lives were always turned toward the river. They fished, and grew manioc in the clearing along its shore. A Sky Eater wandering far into the thick, unnavigable forest was like a faerie wandering into a hawk's hunting territory. It happened only rarely. So when they heard the crashing through the trees, most of the girls screamed. Tiger Lily reached for her hatchet.

Stone came through first, splitting through the branches. The other boys rallied behind him. And Pine Sap, last and weakest of them all, brought up the rear. They were all breathless, shirtless, a muscular and well-organized group with weedy Pine Sap trailing at the back.

Stone gestured for the girls to come with them. "You'll never believe it."

The girls followed the boys through the forest, and I grabbed a tassel of Tiger Lily's tunic because I, too, was curious, and she ran faster than I wanted to fly. And then we cleared the last of the trees leading to the cliffs, and the way to the sea was open, and I heard a noise escape Tiger Lily's lips, a little cry, and heard it on the other girls' lips too as they arrived behind her. There upon the water was a large ship, a skeleton against the sky, collapsed and flailing into the rocks close to shore, broken apart and drowning. The scene was all deep blues and grays and whites and the wild waves lifting it all like deep gasping breaths.

Looking closer, I could see little pink people—tiny, falling and clinging. I knew right away they must be Englanders, a people we knew of from across the ocean.

"They're dying," one of the girls breathed—a reedy thing I knew to be named Moon Eye—gesturing with her thin arms.

Between the ship's decks, the rocks soared. Pieces of it raced into the sea and disappeared. Little people dropped from it in droves.

Pine Sap elbowed Tiger Lily's arm; he pointed, his finger snaking to trace a line farther in. One little rowboat moved toward shore like a water bug, but we could see that it was caught in the breakers.

It had only one occupant—a fragile figure, a lone man. He was making for the shore with all his might and getting nowhere. As we looked on, the waves buffeted him, until finally he was knocked from the boat, though he somehow managed to cling to its bow. He looked to be as good as dead. But seconds later, he hurled himself back on board.

The tiny boat looked fit to capsize, was half full of water already, and the man was not an adept seaman, constantly turning the boat broadwise when it should have been pointed vertically against the waves. Still, he rowed, and rowed, and despite everything, and to our utter surprise, the boat suddenly lurched its way out of the breakers and into the calm waters by the beach. He collapsed down and forward for a moment, as if he might be dead, and then began to row, calmly, toward the shore. Several people in our group let out their breaths. I did too, though no one would have heard me.

To me it seemed like he was trading one deadly place for another, and that drifting back out to sea was no less dangerous than walking into the island without knowing its dangers. The forest would eat him alive, even his bones.

The young people of the tribe were all looking at each other with a combination of exhilaration and fear, except for Tiger Lily, stony and unreadable, her eyes on the man below. Pine Sap grabbed her hand and pulled her back from the cliff's edge; she had been standing so close the wind might have blown her over.

"They'll be deciding what to do about him," Stone said.

Because all Neverlanders knew what danger Englanders brought with them.

The children raced home to see what the village council would do. I stayed and watched the ship floundering in the waves for a while longer, then flew to catch up.

That was the beginning, or at least the beginning of the beginning, of the changes that were coming for Tiger Lily: the arrival of one little man on one little lifeboat. By that day, I had known of Tiger Lily for years. I also knew a little of her history: that Tik Tok, the shaman, had found her while he was out gathering wild lettuce for medicine, under a flower—either abandoned there or hidden from some peril by someone who didn't survive to come back for her. He'd named her Tiger Lily, after the flower she was under, bundled her into his arms, and taken her home. When she'd grown old enough to seem like a real girl, he'd built her a house next to his down the path that led to the woods and moved her into it. He didn't want her borrowing his dresses.

Tik Tok lived in a clay house he'd built himself—the most intricate in the village. It was my favorite home to sleep in when I was passing through, because it had the best nooks, and a faerie always likes to sleep in tight places for fear of predators. He'd seen the same constructions done in one of the other tribes on the island—the Bog Dwellers, who lived in the mud bogs among the old bones of prehistoric animals—and he'd dragged the whole rib cage of a beast home piece by piece to make the frame. With a craftsmanship possessed by no one else in any village, he'd fashioned shelves and windows, to create a dwelling that put the rest of the tribe's simple houses to shame.

Now he was sitting by a warm fire inside, as the sun was setting and the night was growing cool, as it often did at the end of the dry season. He wore a long dress of raspberry-dyed leather—his favorite—and his hair braided down his back, a leather thong tied around his head with a peacock feather in back. His posture was straight and graceful as any woman's. His eyes were closed in concentration, and his lips moved in a conversation with the invisible gods that, as shaman, he visited in trances. Out of breath, Tiger Lily moved into the room soundlessly and hovered, waiting for him to finish.

In a village where everything was uniform and tidy, Tik Tok's house was like a treasure trove. The firelight cast shadows on the curved walls where he kept his curious collection of belongings: tiny bird skulls, feathers, a few stones that looked like any other stones but which he treasured, and a beloved collection of exotic items that had washed ashore over the years, which he had found scouring Neverland's shores. A book, the pages stuck together, the ink blurred. A tarnished metal cup. And, most beloved of all, a box that told time—still ticking away, its mechanism having somehow survived a shipwreck or a long journey across the sea from the continent. The Englanders divided the endlessness of the world into seconds and minutes and hours, and Tik Tok thought this was wonderful.

Tiger Lily moved across the room quietly, examining the clock, the little metal bit he used to wind it, and bending her ear to the loud, steady ticktock, which Tik Tok had renamed himself after in a solemn ceremony attended by the whole village.

Now she sensed a movement, and turned to see that he was observing her.

"Well, my little beast, I hear we have a visitor," he said, looking her up and down with an amused smile. She always managed to look like a wild beast, mud-stained and chaotic. Her hair was constantly escaping her braid to cling to her face, stuck to her, covered in dirt.

"Will we help him?" she asked.

Tik Tok shook his head. "I don't know."

Tiger Lily waited for him to say more, trying her best to remain in respectful silence.

Tik Tok smeared away some of the charcoal he used to line his eyes. "Have you seen my pipe?" he asked.

He stood and moved about the house, searching. He had carved it over two weeks of long intricate work, but it was the fifth one he'd made. He was always losing things. Finally he found it buried under his covers.

He turned his attention to her question, and sighed. Englanders had come to Neverland before. They'd brought their language with them and given it out as a gift to the Bog Dwellers, who had given it to the other tribes in turn over the years. But they'd also brought a strange discomfort to the wild, and they'd been loud and careless in the forest, and gotten themselves murdered by pirates, who hated their fellow Englanders more than anything else on earth and liked to kill them on sight. They'd brought fevers and crippling flus too. But it wasn't any of this that the Sky Eaters feared.

The Englanders had the aging disease. As time went on they turned gray, and shrank, and, inexplicably, they died. It wasn't that Neverlanders didn't know anything about death, but not as a slow giving in, and certainly not an inevitability. This, more than the beasts of their own island, or the brutal pirate inhabitants of the far west shore, was what crept into their dreams at night and chased them through nightmares.

You never could tell when someone would stop growing

old in Neverland. For Tik Tok, it had been after wrinkles had walked long deep tracks across his face, but for many people, it was much younger. Some people said it occurred when the most important thing that would ever happen to you triggered something inside that stopped you from moving forward, but Tik Tok thought that was superstition. All anyone knew was that you came to an age and you stayed there, until one day some accident or battle with the dangers of the island claimed you. Therefore sometimes daughters grew older than mothers, and grandchildren became older than grandparents, and age was just a trait, like the color of your hair, or the amount of freckles on your skin.

It was because of the aging disease, Tiger Lily knew, that the Sky Eaters wouldn't want to help the Englander. They didn't want to catch what he had.

But something about the tiny lone figure, floating from one certain death into another, tugged at her—I could hear it. (As a faerie, you can hear when something tugs at someone. It's much like the sound of a low, deep note on a violin string.)

"He won't survive without our help," Tiger Lily said. "We're supposed to be brave, aren't we?" The wrinkles in Tik Tok's face moved in response. The story they told was familiar to her.

"I'm not a stranger to your love of lost causes, dear one. But you have to be careful who you meet," he said, stoking a pipe thoughtfully. "You can't unmeet them." He took a long drag of his pipe. Being near Tik Tok always gave one the feeling that everything in the world was exactly in the place it ought to be, and that rushing through anything would be an insult and a waste. "And you should be thinking of other things. You're getting too old to run wild like you do. Clean yourself up. Brush your hair. Try to look like a girl."

"I will, if you try to look like a man."

He smiled wryly, because they both knew how impossible that was; he didn't have it in him. Tik Tok was as womanly as a man could ever be, and everyone just accepted it, like they accepted the color of the sky, and the fact that night followed the daytime. Grudgingly, he gave Tiger Lily a puff of his pipe. They sat and watched the colors outside the window. From my perch on a shelf, I inhaled the unfurling wisps as they dissipated: the tobacco made the colors thick, the smells richer. Outside, visible through the window, everyone was dispersing from the fire. The girls were walking ahead and the boys were running to catch up. There was, as always, a dance going on between them, one that I'd never seen Tiger Lily take part in.

She lay on her back and pushed her feet against the wall, wiped a layer of sweat from her neck though the air was chilly. She tapped her feet at the wall in a troubled rhythm.

Tik Tok gave her a knowing look. "You're restless. Everything is too small for you, including your own body. That's what it's like to be fifteen. I remember."

There was a noise in the doorway and they both glanced

up to see Pine Sap, pale, with Moon Eye behind him looking pensive and sorry, the way she often did.

"They've decided to let the Englander die," he said.

I was asleep on a leaf by the main fire when I heard her come out of her hut.

She went to the river to wash, after everyone else had gone to bed. Crocs sometimes made their way this far inland, but I knew she wasn't as scared of them as some of the others, and that she liked to swim alone, after dark. Following her back to her house, I saw there was one candle burning among the huts. Pine Sap's. He was probably up working on a project, or thinking his deep thoughts. I knew, from nights I'd slept in the village, that he was an insomniac.

When Tiger Lily emerged again from her house and into the square, she'd gathered up a bagful of food.

She set out before the sun came up, her arrows strapped to her back.

I watched her go, intrigued, but also sleepy, comfortable and content. I fell back to sleep before I even thought of following her.

Also From
Jodi Lynn Anderson

From Darlington Orchard to New York and Mexico City and back again, Jodi Lynn Anderson's national bestselling series tells the tale of a trio of girls who find friendship and more amid the peach trees of Georgia.